KB141605

김광규 — **상행(上行)**
A Journey to Seoul

한국문학영역총서

A Journey to Seoul

Translated by Brother Anthony, of Taizé
With an Introduction by Kim Young-moo

Original Poems © Kim Kwang-Kyu
Translation © Brother Anthony, Kim Young-moo

Published by Dap Gae Books
#201 Won Bld. 829-22 Bangbae 4-dong, Seocho-gu, Seoul 137-834, Korea
Tel / (02)591-8267, 537-0464, 596-0464   Fax / 594-0464

English Translations of Korean Literature Series

김광규 – 상행(上行)
A Journey to Seoul

Poems by Kim Kwang-Kyu
Translated by Brother Anthony, of Taizé
With an Introduction by Kim Young-moo

도서 출판 답게

머리말

김영무(1944~2001)

김광규는 자신의 글쓰기의 틀로서 아침에 시를 쓰는 버릇을 얘기한 바 있다. 이것은 물론 실제로 오전에 글을 쓰는 생리적 습관을 말하는 것이기도 하겠지만 그의 시를 읽어보면 그것이 단순히 오전에 글쓰는 버릇을 밝히는 것이라기보다는 자신의 시세계의 특질을 은유적으로 암시한 말도 된다는 느낌이 든다. 아침나절에 맑은 정신으로 또박또박 써내려간 것—그것이 바로 김광규의 시편들이다. 그는 처녀시집 『우리를 적시는 마지막 꿈』(1979)의 뒷표지에 적은 글에서 "현실을 있는 그대로 보고 듣고 생각하고 말하는 것은 결코 유보할 수 없는 삶의 권리"라고 얘기한다. 시인이 아침나절 맑은 정신으로 또박또박 쓰는 시는 한편으로는 조작되고 통제된 의식 및 욕망의 거처인 마취상태의 온갖 정체를 밝히는 작업이며 다른 한편으로는 이 몽환상태에서 깨어나는 아픔 속으로 스스로를 또 독자를 초대하는 행위라 하겠다.

1975년 등단 무렵의 초기시들 가운데 〈영산(靈山)〉이 좋은 본보기이다.

내 어렸을 적 고향에는 신비로운 산이 하나 있었다.
아무도 올라가 본 적이 없는 영산(靈山)이었다.

영산은 낮에 보이지 않았다.

산허리까지 잠긴 짙은 안개와 그 위를 덮은 구름으로 하여 영
산은 어렴풋이 그 있는 곳만을 짐작할 수 있을 뿐이었다.

영산은 밤에도 잘 보이지 않았다.
구름 없이 맑은 밤하늘 달빛 속에 또는 별빛 속에 거무스레 그
모습을 나타내는 수도 있지만 그 모양이 어떠하며 높이가 얼마
나 되는지는 알 수 없었다.

내 마음을 떠나지 않는 영산이 불현 듯 보고 싶어 고속버스를
타고 고향에 내려갔더니 이상하게도 영산은 온데간데 없어지고
이미 낯선 마을 사람들에게 물어 보니 그런 산은 이곳에 없다고
한다.

–〈영산〉 전문

이 시는 우리가 흔히 어린시절 및 고향 또는 본질적이고 순수한
그 무엇과 연결시켜 생각하는 이상과 꿈과 동경과 향수의 세계의
허구에서 깨어나는 맑은 정신의 탄생에 관계된 시로 일단 읽을
수 있다. '나'의 느낌이나 생각을 절도있게 다스려 아무런 내색
도 없이 담담하게 이루어지는 이 진술을 읽으면서 우리는 '내'가
마음 속 고향과 신비로운 산의 상실을 가슴아파하고 있는지 어떤
지 헤아리기가 조심스럽다. 그러나 이 영산은 짙은 안개와 구름
에 싸여 있어서 "어렴풋이" 위치만 "짐작할 수 있을 뿐" 밝은 대
낮에도 보이지 않는다는 지적, 어두운 밤 별빛 또는 달빛 속에서
실체의 윤곽이 떠오르는 수가 있지만 모양이나 높이 따위는 알
수 없다는 지적, 또 "아무도 올라가 본 적이 없"었다는 지적에 주

목할 때, 이 시가 보여주는 것은 신비로운 산의 본질이자 동시에 영산의 신비에 도취해 있던 의식이 깨어남으로써 비로소 밝힐 수 있게된 영산의 정체라 하겠다.

이제 깨어있는 맑은 정신으로 현실과 사물에 새로이 눈뜬 시인은 우리에게 고향이란 신비로운 산이 있는 이상화된 어떤 공간도, 고속버스만 타면 곧 갈 수 있는 정다운 어떤 시골도 아님을 안다. "등이 굽은 물고기들"이 역시 "등이 굽은 새끼들 낳고/숨막혀 헐떡이며" 살아가는 "시궁창", 이제는 "떠나갈 수 없는 곳 / 그리고 이젠 돌아갈 수 없는 곳(〈고향〉), 그런 곳이 우리의 고향일 뿐이다. 김광규는 이 숨막히는 오염의 공간, 죽음의 시궁창에 사는 "이미 낯선 마을 사람들"의 뒤틀린 정신과 의식의 모습을 꼼꼼하게 기록하여 보여주는 일에 자신의 시의 많은 부분을 바치고 있다.

김광규의 시가 주로 겨냥하고 있는 독자층 혹은 꼼꼼한 시적 분석의 대상은 일상적인 의미에서의 소시민 중산층이라 보아 무방할 듯하다. 소시민 중산층의 속물근성과 이기주의와 아집을 사회 풍속의 디테일을 통해 구체적으로 파악하여 비판적으로 검토하는 것을 본령으로 삼는 문학 장르가 소설인 바, 김광규의 시세계를 이루는 독특한 산문적·소설적 특징도 그가 본격적인 소설가와 공유하는 이런 핵심적 관심에서 연유하는 것이다. 그리고 김광규가 소시민 계층을 진지한 대화의 상대로 마다하지 않는 까닭이 있다면, 그것은 노동자, 농민, 도시빈민을 포함하는 우리 민족 공동체 구성원 각자의 마음 속에 소시민의 때묻은 모습이 많이 내면화되어 있음을 알기 때문일 터이다. 그들은 결국 우리 자신이 아닌가.

때문은 어른이 된 우리들의 뒤틀린 자화상을 꼼꼼하게 그려 보여주는 데 탁월한 재능을 발휘한 김광규는 또한 이러한 정신의 왜곡과 마비를 강요하는 보다 크고 복잡한 현실의 기본골격을 간결한 구도 속에 정확히 요약 압축하여 제시함에 있어서도 뛰어난 솜씨를 나타낸다. 그가 우리에게 쉬운 말로 똑똑하게 전달하려고 노력하는 유신시대이래 80년대까지 계속되는 갑갑한 현실의 기본구조는 〈어린 게의 죽음〉과 〈매미가 없던 여름〉 또 〈가을 하늘〉이 암시하고 있듯이 무자비한 폭력의 구조이다.

걸기리만 하면 모든 것이 끝장인 무자비한 폭력의 밀림 지대— 양심, 이념, 변명, 후회도 다 쓸데없고 기나긴 세월 동안 갈고 닦은 "아름다운 목청"도 단숨에 목졸려 버리는 공포의 현실로 변한 것이 우리가 살아가는 나라임을 이 시는 극적으로 보여준다. 이러한 폭력과 공포의 현장에서 가위눌린 의식은 한국의 자랑인 파란 가을 하늘을 보고도 두려워서 마음을 조인다.

그렇다면 '발본색원', '일사분란'의 으름장이 으스스한 이런 죽음의 질서는 누가 빚어 놓은 것인가.

그 사람은 작품 〈누군가〉가 명시적으로 밝힌대로 우리가 초대하지도 않았는데 불쑥 나와서 우리의 "진지한 모임"과 "힘찬 발걸음"을 가로막으며 "선량한 이웃을 잡아가고" "우리의 등에 총을 겨누"는 사람이고 "우리의 머릿속으로 들어와 / 큰골에 칼을 꽂고 / 씌어지지 않은 글을 읽"는 사람이기도 하다. 그러나 시인은 이런 침묵과 죽음의 현실에서도 "차가운 광물을 / 몸으로 밀어내며" 비상갱에서 여러 날을 버티며 목숨을 부지하는 광부들처럼 결코 절망하지 않는다. 거기서도 깨어있는 우리의 이런 이웃이 있기 때문이다. 시인이 어둠의 질곡에서도 절망 하지 않고 "몸 속에 퍼지는 암세포까지도 / 우리의 삶으로" 받아들이며 내일 태어날 아이의 이름을 생각한다고 말할 때, 우리가 주목해야 할 한 가지 사실이 있다. 모든 희망과 자유를 위한 싸움은 절망적인 어둠에도 불구하고 "어디선가 이리로 오는 것이 아니라 / 누군가 우리에게 주는 것이 아니라" 절망 속에서 그 절망 때문에 "싸워서 얻고 지켜야 할" 것인 것이다(〈희망〉).

삼라만상은 시간이 흐르면 모두 시들고 죽는다. 사람도 마찬가지이다. 우리도 "짐승처럼 늙어서" 죽는다. 이와 같이 "살아갈수록 변함없는" 것이 우리의 세상이요 삶이다. 그런데 〈오래된 물음〉이 지적하고 있듯이 늘 변함없는 우리의 삶은 죽음을 향한 진행 속에서 거듭거듭 황홀한 아름다움을 창조해냄으로써 몽롱한 졸음에 빠지려는 우리를 흔들어 깨운다. 이 아름다움, 이 향기, 이 꽃은 어디서 오는 것인가. 라일락이 놀랍고 새롭고 더더욱 향기 깊은 것은 그것이 쓰레기에서 피어난 것이기 때문일 터이다.

또한 〈크낙산의 마음〉이 암시하고 있는대로 편안할 수도 있지만 삶답지 못한 삶을 정녕 삶다운 삶이 되게 하는 것은 그 삶의 현장을 떠나 자유로운 삶의 본고장으로 흔히 제시되는 자연에 은거하는 일도 아니다. 근본적으로 가치의 세계인 사람의 세계는 가치라는 중심이 없는 자연과는 다르다. 모든 가치로부터 떠나 있음으로 자유로운 자연상태는 부러운 것이기는 하지만 현실적으로 사람의 몫은 아니다. 그러나 여전히 사람세계의 가치는 이런 자연적 삶의 자유와 자연스러움에 의해 부단히 조명됨으로써만 진정한 가치로 살아날 수 있다.

그러니까 옷을 바꾸어 입듯 어떤 것으로 대치하거나 썩은 이를 빼버리듯 단번에 처치할 수도 없고 그렇다고 산으로 가버리듯 훌쩍 떠나버릴 수 없는 것이 현실의 일그러진 삶이라면, 이 일그러진 현실의 삶을 참되게 바로잡는 일은 그 현실 안에서 어떤 자연스러운 삶의 원리를 회복시키는 일과 관계된다는 것이 김광규의 현실과 삶에 대한 기본인식인 듯하다. 그리고 이런 인식의 호들갑스럽지 않은 범상함이 사람살이의 구체를 냉철히 보고 듣고 판단하는 맑은 의식, 모든 마취상태와 결별한 아침의 맑은 의식과 만나는 곳에서 김광규의 어른스러운 시가 태어난다.

Introduction

by Kim Young-Moo(1944~2001)

Kim Kwang-Kyu has been heard to say that he normally writes his poems in the morning. Of course, he means quite literally that he usually writes his poems before lunch, but at the same time it seems to suggest that one of the main qualities of his writing is the clear-sighted sensitivity of a freshly wakened mind. Kim Kwang-Kyu's poems are trimmed and polished in the morning light after a proper amount of sleep, and an adequate breakfast, they are the fruit of a calm and steady consciousness. In words written for the cover of his first collection of poems(1979) he says 'one of the rights of life, a right that cannot be withheld, is to see and hear and think and speak reality as it is'. That suggests that life should not be 'a pleasant state of anesthesia' but 'a waking pain'. The poem carefully written with morning's clear mind is designed to make clear the true character of the state of anesthesia in which the manipulated and regimented consciousness is at home, and invites readers to feel a pain that awakens from that state of unreal fantasy. A useful introduction to his poetry might be one his very earliest poems, 'Spirit Mountain':

In my childhood village home there was a mysterious mountain. It was called Spirit Mountain. No one had ever climbed it.

By day, Spirit Mountain could not be seen.
With thick mist shrouding its lower half and clouds that covered what rose above, we could only guess dimly where it lay.

By night, too, Spirit Mountain could not be seen clearly.
In the moonlight and starlight of bright cloudless nights its dark form might be glimpsed, yet it was impossible to tell its shape or its height.

One day recently, seized with a sudden longing to see Spirit Mountain — it had never left my heart — I took an express bus back to my home village. Oddly enough, Spirit Mountain had utterly vanished and the unfamiliar village folk I questioned swore that there was no such mountain there.

We may read this as a poem about the birth of a clear mind awakening from the falsehood of the world of ideals and dreams, all the yearning and nostalgia that we tend to experience in connection with childhood and home as well as anything essential and authentic. As we read this poem, that develops so serenely with its 'I' carefully controlling feelings and betraying no emotions or thoughts, we are attentive to reflect in turn whether we too do not somehow suffer from a similar painful loss of a childhood home and its mysterious landscapes.

At the center of the poem stands the mysterious mountain that is somehow there without being there, not visible yet glimpsed, not climbable yet present, and we are invited to perceive in the poem both the nature of the mountain and the mind which it continues to haunt. At one level there is a process of discovery; the spirit mountain is not located in space; it is no use taking a bus and going back to a place that is no longer there, for the mystery of the mountain has to be sought at other levels. The poem certainly does not report a simple loss of illusions; it does invite us to re-examine our evaluations of past experience.

In many of Kim Kwang-Kyu's poems we find this theme of 'no return', often linked to the home and to childhood, but reported with something other than nostalgia. There is at the same time a feeling that the present has betrayed the past, that if the 'unfamiliar people' in the village deny the presence of the spirit mountain now, it is not that they are closer to the truth, but that they have fallen victim to the many forms of alienation present in contemporary society. The village home becomes the symbol of a polluted and shattered national identity.

Pollution and death are everywhere sensed and reported, so that this collection offers an impressive self-portrait of a society in which everyone is reduced, diminished to dwarfish and sub-human proportions. The dominant tone is not a sentimental regret for the past, but a dark satire of the de-humanizing results of those processes which the public authorities often term 'modernization'. As we leave our boring jobs and trail homewards we find ourselves compared to cold-blooded reptiles that in the evening return back to their swamp.

It is one of the achievements of Kim Kwang-Kyu's poems that they have made many aware of the deeper roots of the frequently criticized attitudes of selfishness and compromise that seem at first sight to characterize the modern urban mentality. He explores in his poems topics that are more often the subject of novels and short stories than of lyric verse; here we find the selfish philistinism glimpsed in multiple moments of tiny gestures that strike home. In the end, the 'general reader' is forced to admit that these portraits are only too familiar.

The basic characteristic of the suffocating social atmosphere Koreans experienced from the early 1970s into the 1990s is a constant repetition of merciless violence. Everywhere we look, we find images of a jungle full of a violence that knows no pity: conscience, ideology, exculpation, regret all equally set aside, the cicada is gobbled up by the spider, the long-prepared beautiful voice silenced in a flash by violence and fear. This reality is clearly expressed in many concrete and telling images. Even the cloudless autumn sky of which Koreans are traditionally so proud becomes a symbol and a source of nothing more than trembling anxiety. Purity can so easily be a mere absence of all the irregularities and variety that go to make up a truly human society.

The responsibilities are as clearly indicated as they can be, especially in the poems about life under military dictatorship; yet there is always the hope of resistance to the powers of silence and death; the cactus finally blooms after a long restless stay in the dark. For it is life that triumphs here; the cancer cells within us too are welcomed as part of life, time is spent at night thinking of names for an unborn baby. The struggle against silence and death, the quest for freedom and hope only become more intense, not in a belief that there are always free spirits struggling in spite of oppression and darkness, but because of the surrounding darkness. Hope does not come after despair, but arises because despair presents itself as a possibility and is rejected. What we cannot reject or avoid is the fact of time, of aging and final death; it is insofar as we recognize that our life's course is marked by that finality that we are enabled to create something utterly beautiful. Otherwise we fall asleep, back into anesthesia. We cannot escape the fact that the lilac blooms on a rubbish dump, the lotus flower springs from black slime. Even death itself is best understood as the fate of the seed out of which the new flowers spring.

Real life may not be possible in the daily life of present society, but running up into the unblemished nature of a fictitious Keunaksan Mountain is not at all the solution, for nothing changes there. Nature and human existence follow different laws and values. In nature there are no conflicts of values, but mere being, followed by non-being, and that may be an envious state but what makes life truly human cannot be found there. All that can happen is that the meaning of freedom and nature in human life may, indeed should, be gained by contact with those realities recognized among stones and animals and trees.

Thus the conclusion of these poems for modern humanity is that it is within the present reality that another, dreamed-of reality of freedom and truth has to be constructed by choice and by struggle. And the unfrivolous normality of this vision, Kim Kwang-Kyu's acute discernment as he eagerly examines with eye and ear the stuff of human life, gives us poems in which we encounter a morning mind quite free of all the fumes of anesthesia.

차 례
Contents

未來

19시 30분 서울역 도착
기차 시각표에 적힌 그대로
세련된 상표 붙은 인형들 싣고
서둘러 특급 열차 달려간 뒤
초여름 들판에 빈 철로가 남는다

꼬불꼬불 밭둑길 논둑길 따라
타박타박 걸어가는 어린 여학생
하얀 블라우스 까만 치마
훈풍이 스쳐가고
참으로 헤아릴 수 없는 그녀의 앞날
논물에 얼비쳐 눈이 부시다

Future

Arriving in Seoul at 19:30—
just as it's written in the timetable—
carrying a load of dolls with fancy labels,
the first-class train rushes by and then
empty tracks remain across the early summer plain.

A little school-girl goes plodding along zigzag paths
over banks and dykes,
the breeze stroking her white blouse and black skirt.
How completely unthinkable the life ahead of her is.
Reflected in the water of the paddy-fields,
it dazzles my eyes.

여름날

달리고 싶다
가시덤불 우거진 가파른 산비탈
기관총에 맞은 게릴라처럼
피를 뿜으며
굴르고 싶다
풀에 맺힌 이슬로 혀끝 적시고
새가 되어 계곡 깊숙이
날아 내리고 싶다

넘어지고 싶다
몰려오는 파도에 채여
깎이지 않는 바닷가
한낮의 햇볕 아래 무릎 꿇고
마지막 땀방울까지
흘리고 싶다
바다 밑 깊은 골짜기에
그림자 드리우고
알몸으로 돌처럼
가라앉고 싶다

Summer's day

I want to run.
I want to go rolling down steep mountain slopes
overgrown with brambles, pouring blood
like a guerilla hit by machine-gun fire.
I want to moisten my tongue
in the dew on the grass,
become a bird and fly
deep into a mountain gorge.

I want to go tumbling.
I want to pour out
my last drop of sweat
kneeling under the midday sun
on a shore ever battered by rolling waves
yet never reduced.
I want to sink
naked like a stone
into deep underwater ravines
leaving my shadow behind.

돌아가고 싶다
끈끈한 어둠의 숨결
무더운 수액 출렁이는 숲 속으로
들어가 길을 잃고
헤매고 싶다
쓰러져
잦아들어
땅 속을 흐르고 싶다

I want to go back.

I want to wander,

breathing moist darkness,

back into the forest where sultry sap surges.

After losing my way

I want to totter on,

sink down

and seep into the ground.

어느 志士의 傳記

관청에서는 그를 特異者라고 불렀다.

그는 어렸을 적부터 길바닥에 쓰러진 異教徒를 보살펴 주었고, 젊었을 때는 교활하고 잔인한 强力犯을 옹호했으며, 나이가 들자 불온한 모임에 드나들며 地下運動을 벌였다.

세상은 언제나 亂世였다.

도저히 그는 편안하게 자고, 맛있게 먹고, 돈을 벌어 즐겁게 살 수가 없었고, 또 그래서는 안 된다고 믿었다.

언제나 몸보다 마음을 앞세운 그는 수많은 逸話가 증명하듯 크고 높은 뜻을 지닌 인물이었다.

그러나 死刑臺에 올라가기 전에 聖者처럼 태연할 수 없었던 그는 담배 한 개비와 술 한 잔을 달라고 했단다.

그의 마지막 소원이 이뤄졌는지 나는 모른다.

다만 자기의 몸과 헤어지게 된 순간 그는 큰 소리로 만세를 부르는 대신 연약한 인간이 되어 떨었던 것이다.

그의 志士답지 못한 最後가 나를 가장 감동시킨다.

A patriot's biography

In the government offices they called him a Special Case.

From early childhood he cared for heretics fallen in the streets; as a youth he protected cunning and brutal criminals; then as soon as he was old enough he frequented seditious groups and entered the underground movement.

The times were always turbulent.

There was absolutely no way he could sleep quietly, eat with pleasure, earn money and live happily, and therefore he believed that doing such things was wrong.

Ever preferring heart to body, he pursued a great and lofty goal, as numerous anecdotes testify.

And before mounting the scaffold he, who could never be calm like a sage, requested a cigarette and a glass of wine.

I do not know if his last wish was granted.

But when the moment came for him to part from his body, instead of shouting out defiance boldly, he became a weak human being and trembled.

You know, what touches me most is his end, when he could not act like a patriot.

고 향

등이 굽은 물고기들
한강에 산다
등이 굽은 새끼들 낳고
숨막혀 헐떡이며 그래도
서울의 시궁창 떠나지 못한다
바다로 가지 않는다
떠나갈 수 없는 곳
그리고 이젠 돌아갈 수 없는 곳
고향은 그런 곳인가

Home

Fish with crooked backs
live in the Han River.
Baby fish with crooked backs are born
and though they pant and gasp
they cannot leave Seoul's sewer.
They do not head seawards.
A place you cannot leave,
a place you cannot return to—
is such a place a home?

Note: The Han River flows through Seoul. It has been heavily polluted in recent decades.

봄노래

눈이 녹으며 산과 들
깊은 생각에 잠긴다

희미한 추억을 더듬는 들판
잡초들은 제 키를 되찾고
기억력이 좋은 미류나무
가지마다 꼭 같은 자리에
조심스레 나뭇잎들 돋아난다

진달래는 지난날 생각하며
얼굴 붉히고
산골짝에 풍기는 암내
시냇물은 싱싱한 욕정 흘리고
피임한 여자들은 예쁜
죽음의 아이를 낳는다

이윽고 깊은 생각에서 깨어나
산과 들 조금씩 자라고
남자들은 새로운 아파트를 지으며
고향에서 조금씩 멀어진다

Spring song

As the snow melts, the hills and fields
are plunged deep in thought.

While the plain gropes after vague memories,
its weeds have regained their proper height;
buds are carefully bursting
in just the same spot on each branch
of the poplar trees with their perfect memories.

Azaleas recall days gone by
and blush.
In mountain valleys drifts a scent of rutting,
the streams pour down in fresh passion,
women on the pill give birth to sweet
children of death.

After a while, waking from their thoughts,
mountains and fields gradually grow
while men build new apartment blocks,
becoming that much more estranged from home.

물의 소리

海草처럼 흐느적거리는
산과 들과 나무와 하늘 사이로
보라 황막한 땅 위의 풍경을

안타깝게 날개를 퍼덕이며 새들은 날고
네 발로 거북하게 짐승들은 달리고
바퀴를 굴려 가는 자동차와
바람 속을 떠다니는 비행기들
사람들은 위태롭게 두 발로 걸으며

끝없는 渴症을 술로 빚어 마시고
물을 모방하여 神을 만들고
石油를 파내어 물을 배반하고
낮에는 살을 움직여 얼굴로 웃고
밤에는 둘씩 만나 어색한 장난을 하고
더럽혀진 몸뚱이를 다시 물로 씻는다

버림 받은 金屬의 종족들이여
물기 없는 時間의 불을 피우고
썩어가는 손끝에 침 발라 돈을 세며
평생을 그 곁에서 불충족하라
더욱 많은 죽음을 괴로와하라
물의 축복은 베풀어지지 않는다

The voice of the water

Look what can be seen on the wide stretching earth
between the hills and fields and trees and sky
that sway like seaweed.

Birds fly, pitifully flapping their wings.
Awkward on their four feet, animals trot,
cars roll on wheels,
planes are borne on the wind.
People walk precariously on two feet.

They brew and drink endless thirst that serves as wine.
They make gods in imitation of water
then, unearthing oil, they revolt against water.
By day flesh moved smiles as face,
by night in twos they play clumsy games,
then once again wash their dirty bodies in water.

Tribes of abandoned metal—
may you be dissatisfied a whole lifetime long,
kindling fires of parched time,
spitting on rotting fingertips and counting money.
May you suffer many more deaths.
The blessings of water are not bestowed.

물오리

수직이 아니면서도
가장 곧게 자라는 나무
전기를 일으키지 않는
그 위안의 나뭇가지에
결코 앉지 않는
거룩한 새
오리는 눕거나 일어서지 않는다
겨울 강 물 위를 부드럽게 떠돌며
단순한 몸짓 되풀이할 뿐
복잡한 아무 관습도 익히지 않는다
눈덮인 얼음 속에 가끔
물의 발자국 남기고
지진이 나면 돌개바람 타고
하늘로 날아 오르며
죽음의 땅 위에 화석이 될
마지막 그림자 던지는
완벽한 새
오리가 날아 왔다가
되돌아가는 곳
그곳으로부터 나는 너무 멀어졌다
기차를 타고 대륙을 횡단하고
비행기로 바다를 건너

Ducks

Holy bird!
Never perching
on branches of trees of comfort,
those trees that grow straightest
if not completely vertical,
that generate no electricity.
A duck is not one for lying down or getting up.
Quietly turning in circles on winter rivers,
it merely repeats simple gestures.
It has not picked up any complicated habits.
Sometimes it leaves water prints
in the snow-covered ice
and if an earthquake comes it flies up,
up into the sky, riding the whirlwind,
casting a final shadow
destined to become a fossil
on the land of death.
Most perfect bird!
The place from which the duck comes flying
and to which it returns
is a place I have come too far from.
Borne on trains traversing continents,

나는 아무래도 너무 멀리 와
이제는 아득한 지평을 넘어
되돌아갈 수 없게 되었다
계절이 바뀔 때마다
무심하게 날개치며 돌아가는
오리는 얼마나 행복하랴
그곳으로 돌아가기 위해 나는
애써 배운 모든 언어를
괴롭게 신음하며 잊어야 한다
얻을 때보다 훨씬 힘들게
모든 지식을 하나씩 잃어야 한다
일어서도 또 일어서고 싶고
누워도 또 눕고 싶은
안타까운 몸부림도 헛되이
마침내는 혼자서 떠나야 할 것이다
날다가 죽어 털썩 떨어지는
오리는 얼마나 부러운 삶이랴
살아서 돌아갈 수 없는 곳
그 먼 곳을 유유히 넘나드는
축복받은 새
나는 때때로 오리가 되고 싶다

crossing oceans by plane,

I have traveled so far in any case

that now it is impossible for me

to cross that far horizon and return.

How happy is the duck returning

with unthinking wing-beats

when the seasons change.

If I am ever to return to that place,

I must first forget with groans of pain

all the language I have so arduously learned.

With far greater difficulty than in the gaining

I must lose one by one all the things I know.

Useless the pitiful body's writhing

as it tries to get up and get up again

then lie down and lie down again.

At last I shall have to set out alone.

How enviable then is the life of the duck

that flies and flies then drops—plop—dead.

Blessed bird,

serenely frequenting that far-off place

I can never return to so long as I live.

There are times when I long to be a duck.

도다리를 먹으며

일찍부터 우리는 믿어 왔다
우리가 하느님과 비슷하거나
하느님이 우리를 닮았으리라고

말하고 싶은 입과 가리고 싶은 성기의
왼쪽과 오른쪽 또는 오른쪽과 왼쪽에
눈과 귀와 팔과 다리를 하나씩 나누어 가진
우리는 언제나 왼쪽과 오른쪽을 견주어
저울과 바퀴를 만들고 벽을 쌓았다

나누지 않고는 견딜 수 없어
자유롭게 널려진 산과 들과 바다를
오른쪽과 왼쪽으로 나누고

우리의 몸과 똑 같은 모양으로
인형과 훈장과 무기를 만들고
우리의 머리를 흉내내어
교회와 관청과 학교를 세웠다
마침내는 소리와 빛과 별까지도
왼쪽과 오른쪽으로 나누고

이제는 우리의 머리와 몸을 나누는 수밖에 없어

While eating a flounder

From the earliest days we have always believed
that we resemble God
or that God resembles us.

With an eye and an ear and an arm and a leg
to left and to right, to right and to left
of a mouth eager to speak and genitals eager to be hidden,
we have always compared right with left,
made balances and wheels and raised up walls.

Unable to bear what was not divided,
we divided the freely scattered hills, fields, and sea
between right and left

and in just the same form as our bodies
we made dolls and medals and weapons,
while in imitation of our heads
we erected churches and offices and schools.
Finally we divided even sounds and light and stars
between right and left

and we cannot now help dividing our heads and bodies.

생선회를 안주삼아 술을 마신다
우리의 모습이 너무나 낯설어
온몸을 푸들푸들 떨고 있는
도다리의 몸뚱이를 산 채로 뜯어 먹으며
묘하게도 두 눈이 오른쪽에 몰려붙었다고 웃지만

아직도 우리는 모르고 있다
오른쪽과 왼쪽 또는 왼쪽과 오른쪽으로
결코 나눌 수 없는
도다리가 도대체 무엇을 닮았는지를

So we choose to drink as we eat raw fish.

The flounder trembles and flutters at the strangeness

of our shapes, as we tear at it, eat it alive,

only laughing to observe how both its eyes

are oddly fixed on the right-hand side.

Even now we do not realize

that this flounder simply cannot be divided

into right and left, left and right.

So we do not realize what it might resemble.

Note: trembles and flutters... we eat it alive. Raw fish is a popular dish in Korea as
in other countries. The flesh is detached from the bones and cut into strips while
the fish is still alive. The nervous system of flounders continues to function for a
time after this, so that the dead fish twitches while its flesh is being eaten.

上行

가을 연기 자욱한 저녁 들판으로
상행 열차를 타고 平澤을 지나갈 때
흔들리는 차창에서 너는
문득 낯선 얼굴을 발견할지도 모른다
그것이 너의 모습이라고 생각지 말아다오
오징어를 씹으며 화투판을 벌이는
낯익은 얼굴들이 네 곁에 있지 않으냐
황혼 속에 고함치는 원색의 지붕들과
잠자리처럼 파들거리는 TV 안테나들
흥미 있는 주간지를 보며
고개를 끄덕여다오
농약으로 질식한 풀벌레의 울음 같은
심야 방송이 잠든 뒤의 전파 소리 같은
듣기 힘든 소리에 귀 기울이지 말아다오
확성기마다 울려나오는 힘찬 노래와
고속도로를 달려가는 자동차 소리는 얼마나 경쾌하냐
옛부터 인생은 여행에 비유되었으니
맥주나 콜라를 마시며
즐거운 여행을 해다오
되도록 생각을 하지 말아다오
놀라울 때는 다만
「아!」라고 말해다오

A journey to Seoul

As you pass Pyeongtaek on the way up to Seoul
crossing the evening plains full of autumn smoke,
perhaps in the shaking window you
may glimpse your suddenly unfamiliar face.
Do not think that it is yours!
Are there no familiar faces beside your own,
gnawing dried squid and playing cards?
As you look at the screaming bright roofs
in the twilight and the TV antennas
fluttering like dragon-flies
and your fascinating weekly magazine,
nod your head.
Do not listen to painful sounds
like the calling of grasshoppers
poisoned by pesticides,
like the radio hiss
when the late-night programs are over.
Aren't the energetic songs
played from every roadside loudspeaker cheerful?
And the roar of cars speeding along the motorways?
People have long compared life to a journey.
As you drink your beer or cola,

보다 긴 말을 하고 싶으면 침묵해다오
침묵이 어색할 때는
오랫동안 가문 날씨에 관하여
아르헨티나의 축구 경기에 관하여
성장하는 GNP와 증권 시세에 관하여
이야기해다오
너를 위하여
그리고 나를 위하여

have a pleasant journey.

Do not think at all.

If you are surprised,

say only Ah!

If you want to say more, keep quiet.

When silence feels awkward,

talk about the long drought,

about the football match against Argentina,

about the rising GNP and the stock market.

For your own sake,

and for mine.

Note: The town of Pyeongtaek lies in fertile plains to the south of Suwon, about 2 hours from Seoul on the main railway line to the south.

少額株主의 祈禱

전지전능하신 하느님!

이미 알고 계시겠지만 얼마 전에 고층 건물이 하나 쓰러졌습니다.

강철과 시멘트로 지은 79층, 그 튼튼한 건물이 그처럼 갑자기 무너지리라고는 아무도 생각지 못했습니다. 저도 물론 예외는 아니었습니다. 어느 재벌의 소유인지는 몰라도 도심에 우뚝 솟은 그 빌딩은 멀리 떨어진 우리집에서 바라보아도 저것이 국력이거니 마음 든든했고, 언젠가 나도 주머니 사정이 허락하면 저 꼭대기 스카이 라운지에 올라가 오렌지 쥬스라도 한 잔 마셔보리라 생각했었습니다. 그런데 어느날 갑자기 이 고층 건물이 쓰러진 것입니다.

더구나 그 건물이 우리집 쪽을 향해 쓰러진 덕택으로 그 옥상에 설치되었던 용량 3,000t짜리 냉각탑이 멀리 날아와 우리집에 떨어지며 순식간에 저의 가족과 재산을 앗아가고 말았습니다. 너무나 놀라운 일이라 저는 슬퍼할 겨를도 없습니다. 믿을 수 없는 이 사실 앞에 저는 다만 갈피를 잡을 수가 없을 따름입니다.

아시다시피 저는 선량한 시민이자 모범적 가장으로 평생을 살아 왔습니다.

저의 이력서 및 신원 조회 서류를 참조하면 아시겠지만 저는 여지껏 한번도 이 사회의 법과 질서를 어긴 적이 없습니다. 어려서부터 부모님께 효도했고, 스승을 존경했고, 국방의 의무를 다했으며, 처자식을 사랑했고, 세금을 언제나 기일내에 납부했고,

A small stockholder's prayer

Almighty God!

As you may already know, a high building recently collapsed.

Nobody imagined that such a solid steel-and-cement 79-story building would suddenly fall down like that. I was no exception, of course. Although I didn't know which big corporation it belonged to but only gazed from my distant house at that building, soaring up in the city-center, my heart used to feel safer because we had such a great national resource. I used to think how one day, when funds permitted, I too would go up to the sky-lounge on top and drink at least an orange juice. But then one day that high building suddenly fell down.

Moreover, as that building fell in the direction of my house, the 3000-ton cooling tower on its roof flew off and landed on my home, robbing me in a flash of my family and fortune. It is so astonishing that I have no time to be sad. I simply cannot make any sense of this incredible situation.

As you know I am a law-abiding citizen and have always been a model head of my household.

As you will see if you consult my curriculum vitae and my personal record files, I have until now never failed to observe

신앙 생활을 돈독히 했으며, 여유 있는 대로 저축을 했고, 우리나라에서도 석유가 쏟아져 나오기를 남달리 속으로 기원했습니다. 담배도 피우지 않고, 술도 마시지 않고, 여자를 가까이하지 않으며, 요즘 와서는 커피까지 끊었습니다. 물론 거액의 방위 성금을 낼 처지는 못 되지만 그래도 육교를 오르내릴 때 계단에 엎드린 거지에게 동전 한 개를 던지지 않고 지나간 적은 없습니다.

그런데도 졸지에 가족과 재산을 잃은 저는 천벌을 받았음에 틀림없습니다. 하지만 저는 아직도 알 수가 없습니다. 제가 과연 무슨 천벌을 받을 죄를 지었습니까.

하느님, 저에게 이성을 되돌려주시어 저로 하여금 올바르게 생각할 힘을 주옵소서. 잃어버린 저의 가족과 재산을 정당하게 슬퍼할 능력을 저에게 주옵소서. 그리고 계속하여 약속된 미래, 낙원의 땅을 믿게 하여 주옵소서.

아 멘.

even one of the laws and usages of society. Since childhood I have honored my parents, respected my teachers, done my national service, loved my family, always paid my taxes in due time, been a sincere believer. I put aside savings when I could, and prayed in a special way that they might strike oil in our country too. I don't smoke, I don't drink, I don't go with women, and nowadays I've even stopped drinking coffee. Of course I haven't been able to contribute huge amounts to the National Defense Fund, but still when I use the pedestrian overpass I never go by without tossing a coin to the beggar kneeling on the steps.

Yet there can be no doubt that in suddenly losing family and fortune I am receiving divine punishment. But I cannot imagine what sin I can have committed to deserve this.

God, give me back my reason and give me strength to think correctly. Make me able to grieve properly for my lost family and fortune. And give me enduring faith in the future they promise, a paradise here.

Amen.

수 박

작년 여름에도 그랬었다
매연 자욱한 버스 정류장에서
테레사를 닮은 아주머니는 신문을 팔고
아이들은 고가도로 밑에서
런닝셔츠 바람으로 자전거를 탄다
생선 냄새 비릿한 서울시장 입구
딸기아저씨 리어카에는
얼룩말이 낳은 알처럼
둥그런 수박들이 가득하다
골목길 막다른 집 홍제옥
과부댁은 자식들과 모여 앉아
커다란 수박을 단숨에 먹어 치우고
다시 헛헛한 땀을 흘리며
개장국을 끓이기 시작한다
작년 이 무렵에도 그랬었다
새로운 여름은 오지 않고
밤에도 깊어지지 않고
변함없는 여름만 가 버린다
네모난 수박이 나올 때까지
돌아갈 집도 없이
여름은 언제나 이럴 것인가

Water-melons

It was just the same last year.
Every year at the bus stop,
in air thick with exhaust-fumes,
a woman like Mother Teresa is selling papers
while beneath the elevated highway kids
dressed only in tee-shirt and shorts are riding bikes
and at the fishy entry to the market
the strawberry-man has heaped
his pushcart with round water-melons
looking rather like the eggs a zebra might lay.
At one end of an alley is a tavern where
a widow and her children have sat down together
and rapidly devoured a huge water-melon,
then still sweating hungrily begin to prepare dog stew.
It was just the same this time last year.
No new summer ever comes.
By night the summer gets no deeper;
unchanged the summer simply ends.
So maybe having no home to return to,
summer will always be like this,
until melons grow square?

바닷말

미역 냄새 싱싱하게
밀려오는 바닷가
해를 싣고 돌아온
고깃배 닻을 내리고
모래톱에 퍼지는 아침 햇살
밤새도록 바다를 건너 와
파도는 섬세하게 부서지며
부드러운 몸짓 끝내고
강아지를 앞세운
어린이와 아낙네들
물을 차며 달려간다
갈매기는 끼룩대며 맴돌고
펄떡이는 도미와
꿈틀대는 장어들
해삼과 소라는 아직도
물 속의 꿈에 젖어 있다
생선값이 얼마냐고 묻지 말고
물가에 널려진 바닷말을
우리의 몫으로 줍자
그리고 깊은 바다의 진주가
먼 도시로 팔려 가기 전에
되돌려 주자

Seaweed

The seashore is swept by a fresh tang
of brown seaweed.
A fishing boat bringing back the sun
drops anchor and morning light spreads across the sand
having spent the night crossing oceans.
Waves break softly
bringing their soft motion to an end while,
with a little dog leading the way,
women and children
go running along kicking up the water.
As gulls wheel screaming,
flapping sea-bream
and wriggling eels
with sea-slugs and shellfish
are still sunk deep
in their watery dreams.
Let's not ask the price of fish
but gather up the seaweed
scattered across the shore for our share
and before the deep-sea pearl
can be sent to the distant city for sale
let's return

어부들에게 살아 있는 고기를
고기들에게 숨쉬는 바다를

living fish to the fishermen,

the breathing sea to the fish.

450815의 행방

오늘은 광복절, 공휴일이자 토요일, 유달리 더운 올 여름의 마지막 연휴입니다. 우리들은 다투어 도시를 떠나 물가로 달려가거나 산에 올라가 즐겁게 하루를 보낼 것입니다.

당신과 함께 잊혀진 그 날은 언제던가요.

힘차게 솟아오르는 아침해를 등지고 당신은 서쪽으로 먼길을 떠났습니다. 우람한 그림자는 거인처럼 앞장서 당신을 인도했지요.

당신은 부지런히 걷고 숨가쁘게 뛰었습니다.

한낮의 고개 위에 그림자를 밟고 서서 당신은 자랑스럽게 땀을 씻었지요. 정상에서 모든 시간이 멈출 수 있다면 우리들은 당신과 헤어지지 않았을 것입니다.

서녘으로 비껴 가는 내리막길에서 어느새 하나 둘 낙엽이 지고, 당신을 바짝 뒤쫓던 그림자도 힘을 잃고 늘어져 발걸음을 무겁게 했습니다.

마침내 눈덮인 들판의 저녁 노을이 몸을 적실 때, 그림자는 지쳐서 당신을 떠나 버리고 당신은 혼자서 어둠의 나라로 들어섰습니다. 눈부신 어둠 속에 당신은 비로소 걸음을 멈춘 것입니다.

산비둘기가 가끔 솔밭에서 울고 까치들이 내려앉아 깃털을 다듬는 무덤 곁에 당신은 온종일 무료하게 그림자도 없이 앉아 있었지요.

Missing person: Born August 15, 1945

Today is National Liberation Day, a Saturday and a holiday, the last long weekend of this particularly hot summer. We shall all fight to get out of the city and hurry to the seaside or up a mountain to spend a pleasant day.

When can that day have been? I have forgotten it along with you.

Turning your back on the fiercely beating rays of the rising sun, you set out on your long journey westwards. And a sturdy shadow like that of a giant was there before you, guiding you on.

You walked briskly and ran panting.

On a midday crest you stood trampling your shadow and proudly wiped away the sweat. If only we could have stopped the flow of time up there, we would surely never have been parted.

On the slanting downhill path in a flash the leaves had fallen and the shadow dogging you had lost its strength too and drooped along, burdening your footsteps.

Finally, when twilight on the snow-covered plains had soaked you through, your exhausted shadow abandoned you and you went on alone into the realms of night. You only came

때로는 빛바랜 혼령이 되어 박쥐가 날아다니는 꿈 속에 나를 찾아오기도 했고.

그날 갑자기 당신은 우리집 마당으로 들어섰습니다. 낯익은 허리띠를 매고, 조그만 아기가 되어 조그만 그림자를 이끌고, 해맑은 웃음을 지으며 내 앞에 나타났습니다.
앞서 간 당신은 누구였습니까. 이제 나를 뒤따라오는 당신은 누구입니까. 그리고 오늘은 언제인가요.

to a halt once enclosed in the dazzling dark.

Then you would sit the whole day long idly without even a shadow, beside the tomb where the pigeons called and the magpies came down to preen their feathers.

Sometimes, becoming a faded ghost, you would visit me in bat-fluttering dreams.

One day you suddenly entered the courtyard of our house. Now a tiny child, with a tiny shadow, wearing your familiar belt, smiling bright as the sun, you appeared before me.

Who are you, who went on ahead? Who are you, who now follow along behind me? And when is today?

Note: August 15, 1945. The date of the Japanese surrender, on which it undertook to withdraw from all the territories it had occupied on the continent of Asia, including Korea. What should have been a restoration of proud independence instead degenerated into the tragedy of the Korean War and the enduring division of the peninsula.

二 代

관리들에게도
관복을 입히던 시절
중문 밖 행랑채에는
강서방 내외가 살았다
어멈은 물을 긷고
아범은 인력거를 끌었다
주인집 일을 거들지만
밥은 따로 해 먹었다

학생들의 교복도
사라진 오늘
운전기사 강씨네는
차고에 딸린 두 칸짜리
연탄방에서 산다
마누라는 안집의 빨래를 해 주지만
밥은 따로 해 먹는다
미스터 강은 메르체데스를 끌고

Two generations

In the old days,

when even state officials wore uniforms,

the Kangs lived, husband and wife,

in the servants' quarters in the outer compound.

The woman drew water,

the man was yoked to a rickshaw,

both worked for the master's house

but they cooked and ate apart

Today,

when even school uniforms have disappeared,

driver Kang and his wife

live in a nine-foot-long room

attached to the garage.

The wife does the washing for the main house

but they cook and eat apart

and 'Mister' Kang is yoked to a Mercedes.

4월의 가로수

머리는 이미 오래 전에 잘렸다
전기줄에 닿지 않도록
올해는 팔다리까지 잘려
봄바람 불어도 움직일 수 없고
토르소처럼 몸통만 남아
숨막히게 답답하다
라일락 향기 짙어지면 지금도
그날의 기억 되살아나는데
늘어진 가지들 모두 잘린 채
줄지어 늘어서 있는
길가의 수양버들
새잎조차 피어날 수 없어
안타깝게 몸부림치다가
울음조차 터뜨릴 수 없어
몸통으로 잎이 돋는다

Roadside trees in April

Their tops were cut off long ago
so as not to touch the power lines.
This year even their limbs have been lopped
so they cannot sway if a spring breeze blows
and only the trunks remain like torsos
suffocating and grim.
When the lilac perfume deepens,
memories of another April day return
but now every trailing branch has been cut off
so that the street-side weeping willows,
lined up in rows,
unable even to put out new leaves,
seething with impatience but
unable to utter even a cry,
are putting out leaves from their trunks.

5월의 저녁

신록의 바람 타고
우울한 소식
어느 집에선가 들려오는
서투른 피아노 소리

바크하우스는 벌써 죽었고
루빈슈타인도 이미 늙었는데
어른들의 절망 아랑곳없이
바이에르 상권을 시작하는 아이들

신문지에 싸서 버릴 수 없는
희망 때문에
평온한 거리마다
부끄럽게 나리는 어둠

Evening in May

Borne on the early summer breeze,
gloomy news.
Emerging from some house or other,
clumsy piano sounds.

Backhaus is already dead,
now Rubinstein is getting old,
but regardless of adults' despair
there are children beginning Bayer I

and because of this hope that cannot be
wrapped up in newspaper and thrown away,
darkness drops shamefaced
down every quiet street.

Note: This poem was written as a commentary on the tragic events in Gwangju (South Jeolla Province) in May 1980.

어떤 고백

나는 몰지각한 남자였는지도 모른다. 여자가 되고 싶었으니 말이다.

매일 수염을 깎아야 한다든지, 여름에도 긴 바지를 입고 땀을 흘려야 한다든지, 나라를 지키면서 돈을 벌어야 한다든지 이런 것들이 싫어서가 아니었다.

아무나 사랑해도 안 되고, 아무나 싫어해도 안 되고, 그렇다고 가만히 있을 수도 없고, 이기지 못하면 지는 수밖에 없는 남자 노릇이 싫어졌기 때문이었다.

그러나 정작 여자가 되어 이 세상의 모든 남자들을 — 대학생, 부두 노동자, 농민, 막벌이꾼, 실직자, 경찰, 범죄자, 엔지니어, 선원, 고물장수, 군인, 정치가, 상인, 브로커 등을 가리지 않고 몸소 사랑하자 남자들은 나를 화냥년이라 불렀고, 여자들은 나에게 침을 뱉었다.

남자들의 관습과 여자들의 질서를 지키지 않은 죄로 하마터면 감옥에까지 끌려갈 뻔했다. 여자 노릇은 더욱 힘든 것 같았다.

이제는 남자도 아니고 여자도 아닌, 즉 사람이 아닌 무엇이 되고 싶었다.

그리하여 지난 봄에 나는 한 마리의 개가 되었다. 네 발로 달리는 것이 두 발로 뛰는 것보다 훨씬 빠르다는 사실을 새삼 느낄 무렵 계절은 여름으로 접어들었다.

A kind of confession

Perhaps I was a thoughtless kind of man? I mean I wanted to become a woman.

Not because I had to shave every day, or wear long pants even in summer and sweat, or defend the nation and earn money, not for that kind of reason.

But because I detested the role of a man, not allowed to love anybody, or detest anybody, and not just to keep quiet either, and if you don't win you lose.

But then when I really became a woman, I loved all the men of the world—students, stevedores, farmers, day-laborers, loafers, policemen, criminals, engineers, seamen, second-hand dealers, soldiers, politicians, tradesmen, brokers, and all, indiscriminately, and they called me a whore, while the women spat at me.

I only just escaped being dragged off to prison for not observing men's customs and women's proper place. A woman's role seemed even more difficult.

So then I wanted to become something that was neither man nor woman, that is to say not human.

So last spring I became a dog. Just as I was discovering how

사람들은 닥치는 대로 개들을 잡아다 두들겨 죽이고 끓는 보신
탕 솥에 집어넣었다. 수많은 나의 동족들이 순전히 재수가 나빠
목숨을 잃었다.

이 길고 지긋지긋한 여름을 한번 짖어 보지도 못하고 숨어서
견뎌낸 것은 결코 나의 능력이 아니었다. 아직도 살아 있기는 하
지만 나는 이미 개다운 개도 못 된다.

보신탕을 먹지 않는 나라, 개들의 천국은 어디 있는가.

much faster you can go on four feet than on two, summer came.

People casually caught dogs, killed them with a blow and tossed them into seething pots. Many of my fellows lost their lives by sheer bad luck.

It was by no skill of mine that I managed to survive that long dreadful summer, hidden without being able even to bark once. I am still alive, but I can never become a dog-like dog.

I wonder, might there somewhere be a land where they don't eat dog—a dogs' Paradise?

Note: This poem was written as a veiled commentary on the establishment of the new military dictatorship of Chun Doo-Hwan during the summer of 1980.

목발이 김씨

지하 5층
지상 30층
연건평 35000평
서울빌딩 기초 공사 때
김씨는 막일을 했다
현기증나는 비계를 오르내리며
자갈을 져나르고
미장을 돕고
타일을 붙이고
창틀을 달았다
서울빌딩 주춧돌 밑에는
김씨의 고된 인생이 3년쯤
깔려 있고
하늘로 꼬여 올라간
아찔한 비상 계단 어디엔가
김씨의 잃어버린 왼쪽 다리
걸려 있다

안전모를 착용한 덕분에
그래도 목숨은 건져
반년 만에 김씨가 목발 짚고
병원을 나왔을 때

Kim with crutch

5 basement levels
30 floors above ground
150,000 square yards of floor space—
when they were doing the groundwork
for Seoul Building
Kim did the rough jobs.
Up and down the dizzying scaffolding
he carried loads of gravel
he helped with the plastering
he stuck on tiles
he fixed window-frames.
Under Seoul Building's foundation stone
lie some 3 years of Kim's hard life
and somewhere up the dizzying emergency stairs
that go snaking heavenwards
is stuck
the left leg Kim lost there.

Luckily he was wearing a safety helmet
so he escaped death by a hair
and six months later
when Kim came out of hospital on crutches

우뚝 솟은 서울빌딩은
장안의 명물이 되었다
없는 것 없는 백화점과
잠을 자기에는 너무 아까운 호텔
사우나탕과 레스토랑과 금융회사 사무실들
어디서나 하얀 남자들이
재빠르게 계산기를 두드리고
암나사처럼 생긴 여자들이
껌을 짝짝 씹으며
지난 밤을 생각하고
시간도 돈으로 팔고 사는
그곳은 살아 있는 TV 화면이었다

발을 헛딛고
추락했던 그 자리
13층 비상 계단 입구는
어떻게 마무리되었는지
오직 그것이 보고 싶어 김씨는
다리를 절룩이며
옛날의 일터를 찾아갔다
용접공 이씨를 만나면
반가워 낮술 한잔

Seoul Building towering aloft

had become a well-known feature of the capital.

Department stores with every kind of everything,

a hotel too luxurious to sleep in,

saunas and restaurants and financial company offices,

everywhere white-clean men

busily banging away on computers,

girls looking like screw-holes

noisily chewing gum

and recalling last night,

with time too bought and sold for cash,

it was a TV screen come alive.

Wanting only to see how that spot

at the entrance to the emergency stairs

on the 13th floor

where he had tripped and gone headlong

had been finished off,

Kim went hobbling along

to visit his former work-site.

Suppose he happened to meet Lee the welder,

then they might down a daytime glass

꺾을지도 모른다
그러나 서울빌딩 현관 앞에서
넥타이를 맨 수위가
그를 가로막았다
일없는 사람은 들어갈 수 없다고
쓰레기를 쳐 가는 뒷문에서도
험상궂은 문지기가 길을 막았다
김씨는 돌아서서
어디로 가나

to celebrate.

But at the entrance to Seoul Building

a janitor wearing a necktie

stopped him,

saying 'People without work can't come in here,'

and at the back door where the garbage goes out

a fearsome guard blocked his path.

So Kim turned away.

Who knows where he went?

야바위

동전은 다섯 개뿐
던지면
결과는 뻔하다
앞
아니면
뒤

그래도 속임수로
섞고
바꾸고
던지고
받고

순열과 조합 다 해 봐도
달라질 수 없어
돈을 대면
눈깜짝할 사이에
물주가 먹어 버린다

눈을 비비고
다시 보아도
동전은 다섯 개뿐

Trickery

Just five coins.
If you toss them
the result is obvious—
heads
or
tails

yet by deception
mixed
exchanged
tossed
picked up

though you try all kinds of permutations
you can do nothing about it:
if you put down your money
in the time it takes to blink
the banker has grabbed it.

Rub your eyes
and look again—
still just five coins

앞
아니면
뒤

달라진 것은 없다
누가 돈을 먹는가
그것밖에는

heads

or

tails

nothing has changed,

only the question:

Who's grabbing the money?

物神素描

그는 보통사람이 아니다
결코 평범한 사람이 아니다
보통사람보다 훨씬 너그럽고
평범한 사람보다 훨씬 잔인한 그는
괴로움을 참으며 짐짓
눈물을 감추는 연약한 사람이 아니다
달을 바라보며 지난날을 그리워하는
그런 사람이 아니다
가슴 조이는 관중들 앞에서
골키퍼처럼 날쌔게 볼을 잡아낸
그는 온종일 일하고
저녁때 퇴근하는 사람이 아니다
교통순경이 무서워 차선을 지키는
그런 사람이 아니다
쓸 만한 말들을 혼자서 골라갖고
하얀 침묵의 항아리를 빚어낸 그는
말로 이야기하는 사람이 아니다
끝없이 밀려오는 파도를 바라보며
바다의 마음을 헤아리는
그런 사람이 아니다
믿을 수 있는 것은 오직 하나
어제의 나뿐이라 생각하며

Sketch of a fetish

He is no common man,

definitely not an ordinary man.

Far more lenient than a common man

far crueler than an ordinary man,

he is not some meek kind of man

who endures hardship patiently,

deliberately hiding his tears.

He is not a man who gazes at the moon,

longing for days gone by.

Nimbly seizing the ball

like a goalkeeper before a tense crowd,

he is not a man who works all day

and then goes home in the evening.

He is not the kind of man who keeps to his lane

for fear of the traffic patrols.

He is not a man who speaks in words

as he takes over all the best expressions,

producing an urn of white silence.

He is not someone who gazes

at the endlessly rolling waves

and fathoms the ocean's heart.

He is not a man who hastens

새벽길을 달려가는 사람이 아니다
고개를 숙이고 말없이 따라가는
그런 사람이 아니다
거룩한 짐을 힘겹게 짊어지고
언제나 앞서 가는 그는
결코 평범한 사람이 아니다
보통사람이 아니다
한 마디로 그는 사람이 아니다

onwards at dawn firm in the conviction

that yesterday's I is alone believable.

He is not the kind of man who lowers his head

and silently follows after.

Taking up sacred burdens beyond his power

and marching on and on, he is definitely

not an ordinary man, not a common man,

in short not a man at all.

얼굴과 거울

울퉁불퉁한 거울을 들여다보면
눈이 턱 아래로 내려가고
코가 눈 위로 올라가고
귀가 머리 위로 뿔처럼 솟아오르고
드라큘라처럼 송곳니가 삐드러져 나온다
우리의 얼굴이 정말로 그렇게 생겼는가
아니면 이것은 거울이 잘못된 때문인가

눈이 턱 아래 붙어 있고
코가 눈 위에 달려 있고
귀가 머리 위에 뿔처럼 솟아 있고
송곳니가 삐드러져 나온 드라큘라가
울퉁불퉁한 거울을 들여다보면
아주 반듯한 사람의 모습이 된다
드라큘라의 얼굴이 정말로 그렇게 생겼는가
아니면 이것은 거울이 잘못된 때문인가

너무나도 보잘것없는 소원이지만
사람에겐 사람의 모습을
드라큘라에겐 드라큘라의 모습을
그대로 보여 주는 거울을 갖고 싶다

Face and mirror

If you look into a bumpy mirror,
down drop the eyes beneath the chin,
up goes your nose above the eyes,
an ear sprouts like a horn on top of your head
and your canines stick out like Dracula's.
Do our faces really look like that?
Or is it all the mirror's fault?

If a Dracula with eyes beneath his chin
and a nose stuck on above his eyes,
an ear sprouting like a horn on top of his head
and with canines sticking out
looks into a bumpy mirror,
his appearance becomes that of a handsome fellow.
Does Dracula's face really look like that?
Or is it all the mirror's fault?

It's really a trifling wish, I know,
but how I long to have a mirror
in which people look like people
and Dracula looks like Dracula.

잊혀진 친구들

늦잠에서 깨어나 목욕하고 마시는 향긋한 커피 맛을 그들도 잘
안다.

귀여운 꼬마들을 데리고 어린이 대공원에서 즐거운 일요일을
보낸 적도 있다.

차가운 굴을 놓고 뜨거운 청주를 마시던 겨울 바닷가를 그들도
기억한다.

그러나 이제는 안부도 물을 수 없는 곳에 가 있는 사람들이 그
들 가운데 많다.

어떤 친구는 용돈이 없어 담배를 끊었고, 어떤 친구는 홧김에
술만 더 늘었다.

섣불리 사업에 손을 댄 그는 전세집까지 홀랑 날리고, 지난 가
을부터 강남의 어느 복덕방에 나간다고 한다. 바둑은 많이 늘었
지만 먹고 살기가 어려운 모양이다.

머리를 깎고 절에 들어가 중이 되려고 했다가 간첩 혐의로 몰
려 혼이 난 친구도 있다.

마누라가 선생 노릇을 하는 덕택에 아도르노를 번역하겠다고
집 속에 틀어박힌 그는 오랜만에 나와보니 맹꽁이처럼 배가 나
왔다.

Forgotten friends

They too know the taste of fragrant coffee drunk after taking a bath on waking up late.

They too have spent happy Sundays in the Children's Park with cute infants in tow.

They too recall the autumn seaside where we ate cold oysters and drank warm rice wine.

But nowadays many of them are among those who have gone to places you cannot expect to get any news from.

One friend stopped smoking for lack of pocket money, another only drank more out of spite.

Another went into business and lost his house but since last autumn he's working in a house-agent's south of the river. He's got better at checkers but has a hard time making ends meet.

There is also the friend who had a bitter experience: he cut off his hair to become a monk, only he got arrested on suspicion of being a spy.

One, thanks to his wife's work as a teacher, closeted himself at home and said he was going to translate Adorno. When I met him again his stomach was sticking out like a fat frog's.

구두닦기를 하는 것도 그렇지만, 길가에 포장마차를 차리는 것도 보기와는 달리 아는 사람이 없으면 힘들단다.

이발소를 냈다가 실패하고, 월부책을 팔다가 때려치우고, 택시를 몰다가 사고를 내고, 마지막으로 장의사를 개업하겠다고 벼르던 그 친구는 국민학교 4학년짜리를 남겨 놓은 채 간장염으로 죽고 말았다.

세상은 이성을 잃고 너무나 오랫동안 그들을 잊었다.

그리고 손 끝에서 피 한 방울만 나도 파상풍균을 생각하는 사람들이 남아서 신문에 난 아야톨라 호메이니의 사진을 들여다보고 이란의 앞날을 걱정한다.

Cleaning shoes is hard of course, but they say that despite appearances setting up a street-side bar is hard too unless you know the right people.

One friend opened a barber's shop and failed, sold monthly magazines but gave it up, drove a taxi but had an accident, finally he was expressing an intention of becoming an undertaker only he succeeded in dying of hepatitis first, leaving one child in fourth grade.

The world has lost its mind and forgotten them all for far too long.

Only people who think of tetanus germs as soon as they see a drop of blood welling at the tip of a finger feel concerned about the future of Iran, on seeing pictures of the Ayatollah Khomeiny in the papers.

1981년 겨울

낮과 밤이 하나로
검은 땀 되어
숨가쁘게 흘러내리는
지하 300m
막장에서 갑자기
물줄기가 터졌다
쏟아져 나오는 죽탄
순식간에 갱도를 막아 버린
시커먼 죽음
그 차가운 광물을
몸으로 밀어내며
하루 이틀 사흘
비상갱에서 겨우 목숨을
건졌을 때 비로소
시간이 다시 흐르고
목숨은 거듭 태어났다

힘겹게 견뎌 온 우리의 삶을
1분도 멈출 수 없는
시뻘건 목숨을
낙서처럼 지워 버린 그것은
결코 기계의 잘못이 아니다

Winter 1981

A flood of water
exploded suddenly, spouting
into mine galleries
300 yards underground
where day and night blend,
breathlessly pouring
in a single black sweat.
Black death, the spurting liquid coal
filled the shafts in a flash
but some fought against
the chill mine-water
for one day, two days, three,
barely surviving
in emergency shafts. Then
time flowed again,
life was reborn.

That event, rubbing out lives
like scribbles,
our lives of weary pain,
crimson lives that cannot
for one minute rest,

컴퓨터에 자료를 넣은
그들의 잘못도 아니고
그들에게 지시한
그 사람의 잘못도 아니다
그 사람이 받은 명령은
아득히 먼 곳에서 왔다
어딘가 너무 멀어
보이지 않는 그 곳은
우리의 머리 속에
가슴 속에
마음 속에도 있다

눈 감고
귀 기울이면
가파른 산을 넘고
녹슬은 철조망을 지나
우리를 찾아오는 바람 소리
육신을 잃고
휘파람으로 떠도는 말들이
허공을 할퀴며 달려들어
혀를 찌른다
거리마다 침묵의 구호들

was certainly no mechanical error.

Nor was it an error

on the part of those feeding data

into the computer

or an error of the one

who gave them their instructions.

The orders he received

came from a distant place, too far away

for us to see where it lies.

That place lies in our heads, in our breasts

and in our hearts as well.

If we close our eyes

and listen hard to

the sound of the wind

crossing steep mountains

and passing through rusty fences to reach us,

stripped of flesh and blood,

whistling words wandering

come clawing at the air

and sting the tongue.

In every street slogans of silence

시체처럼 널려 있고
상점마다 바겐세일의 깃발
만장처럼 펄럭이는데
자유를 자유라 부르며
사랑을 사랑이라 부르는
우리의 모국어는 어디 있는가

온종일 들려 오던
호각 소리 멈추고
유리로 된 진열장이
모두 닫힌 밤
우리는 잠들지 않고
깨어 있었다
심장의 고동 헤아리며
앞으로 태어날 아이의
이름을 생각했다
동이 트면 또다시
어제의 옷을 입지만
이제는 쫓기며 뛰지 않겠다
안개낀 새벽길을
천천히 걸으며
잊었던 말들을 되살리고

lie scattered like corpses

and on every store-front bargain-sale signs

flap like so many funeral banners

but tell me, where now is our mother tongue

that calls freedom freedom,

that calls love love?

Evening comes and the whistle

we have heard all day falls silent,

the glassed-in shop fronts

are all closed.

We did not sleep

but lay awake

and counting the heart-beats

thought of names

for the baby soon to be born.

Once again when day dawns

we shall put on yesterday's clothes

but now we will not run on command.

We'll go walking slowly

along early morning misty roads,

bringing forgotten words back to life,

몸 속에 퍼지는 암세포까지도
우리의 삶으로
받아들이겠다

and accept even the cancerous cells

spreading in our bodies

as part of life.

손가락 한 개의

우연히 마주친 눈길이
나침처럼 한동안 떨렸다
열린 채 닫혀 있는 곳
팽팽하게 가득 채우며
끝없이 깊게 그러나
손가락 한 개의 길이로
겹쳤을 때
온 세상이 몸을 뚫고
뜨겁게 지나갔다
지나간 세상의 어느 곳엔가
가 버린 시간의 언제쯤엔가
아슴푸레 눈길 멈추고
목 매달려
한동안 지났을 때
끝없이 멀리 그러나
손가락 한 개의 사이를 두고
땅에 닿을 듯 말 듯 두 발이
차갑게 늘어졌다

One finger's length

Eyes meeting by chance
trembled for a moment like compass needles.
A space once open was now shut,
filled up tightly,
endlessly deeply yet
when we overlapped
by a single finger's length
the whole world pierced
and passed burning through.
Somewhere in the world gone by,
once for a moment in time now lost,
as dull eyes stood riveted,
throats tightening,
a moment passed
endlessly distant yet
with only one finger's length between them,
unsure if they touched the ground or not
as two pairs of feet trailed indifferently.

가을 하늘

구름 한점 없이
파란 가을 하늘은
허전하다
땅을 덮은 것 하나도 없이
하늘을 가린 것 하나도 없이
쏟아지는 햇빛
불어오는 바람

하늘을 가로질러
낙엽이라도 한잎 떨어질까봐
마음 조인다

얼마나 오랫동안
저렇게 견딜 수 있을까
명령을 받고
싹 쓸어 버리기라도 한 듯
구름 한점 없이
파란 가을 하늘은
두렵다

Autumn sky

Not a single cloud.
The blue autumn sky
looms empty—
nothing covering the earth,
nothing veiling the sky,
sunlight pouring down,
the wind blowing.

My heart is on edge.
Suppose a dead leaf should fall
across the sky?

I wonder how long
it can endure?
As if on a word of command,
everything has been swept clean away
and without a single cloud
the blue autumn sky
looms fearful.

책노래

혁명이란 위험한 짓
금지된 장난이다
그러나 역사를 보라
일찍이 끔찍한 혁명이 없이
위대한 나라
새로운 시대가
탄생한 적 있는가

위대한 생각을
새로운 언어로
기록한 것이 훌륭한 책이라면
그것은 앞으로 역사를 이끌어갈
머리의 힘
마음의 꿈이다

그러나 혁명을 일으킨 자들은
언제나 혁명을 가장 두려워하고
천성이 책을 좋아하지 않아
훌륭한 책을 읽는 대신
금지할 책을 골라낸다

A song about books

Revolution's a dangerous thing,
a forbidden game,
but only consider history—
has there ever been a single instance
where a great nation or a new age
has come to birth
without a terrible revolution?

If something containing a wonderful idea
in a new language
is what is called a great book,
it is the power of the mind,
the dream in the heart
that will lead history forward.

But the people who launch revolutions
are always those who most fear revolutions
and their natural disposition being to dislike books,
instead of reading great books
they reflect on which books to ban.

그리하여 책을 금지한 자들은
생각과 느낌마저 금지하고
〈책을 불태운 자들은
마침내 사람마저 불태우고〉
결국은 스스로 파멸한다
역사를 돌이켜보라
禁書와 焚書는 혁명보다도
위험한 장난 아닌가

Now the people who ban books

are really banning thought and feeling:

'the people who burn books

are in the end really burning people'

and as a result they bring themselves down.

Just think back through history.

Are not book-banning and book-burning

even more dangerous games than revolutions?

이사장에게 묻는 말

가슴 가득히 훈장을 단 당신은
담배를 피우며 회고했다
「그것은 나의 잘못이 아니었다
전쟁터에서는 아군이 아니면 적군이다」
명령을 내리기 전에 당신이
파이프를 한 대 더 태웠더라면
오늘이 조금 달라졌을까

아침마다 승마를 하고
주말에는 골프를 치면서
요즘도 당신은 퇴역 사성 장군은
이 세상의 모든 사람을
적 아니면 동지라고
믿고 있는가

그렇다면 복덕방 김 영감은
적인가 동지인가
오너드라이버가 된 이 과장은
엘리베이터를 기다리는 미스 박은
도서관에 가득한 저 학생들은
과연 동지인가 적인가
공판장의 정 서방은

To the Chairman of the Board

Your chest covered with medals, you
smoked a cigarette as you brooded on the past.
'That was no fault of mine.
On the battlefield you are either friend or foe.'
If only you had smoked another pipe
before you gave the orders,
wouldn't today have been a little different?

Don't you still consider
every person in this world
either an enemy or a friend,
as you go off horse-riding every morning
with a round of golf at weekends,
now you are an honorably retired general?

In that case is Mister Kim from the housing agency
friend or enemy?
And section-head Lee who now drives his own car,
Miss Park there waiting for the elevator
or all those students crowded in the library,
are they friend or enemy?
And Mr. Chong from the co-operative market,

생산부의 최 기사는
거동이 수사한 저 청년들은
적인가 동지인가
거리에 정거장에 백화점에 넘치는
저 많은 사람들은
그리고 지금은 이사장이 된 당신 자신은
도대체 동지인가 적인가

engineer Choe from the production department

or those youngsters with their suspicious activities,

are they enemy or friend?

And what of all those people

crowding the streets, the stations, the shops

and you yourself now become Chairman of the Board,

for heaven's sake, enemy or friend?

새 문

일년에 한번쯤 한 사람이
드나들기 위하여
저렇게 커다란 정문을
한가운데 만들어 놓고
열두 명의 수위가 밤낮으로 지킨다
〈정문 사용 금지〉
보통사람들은 절대로
드나들 수 없는
저 으리으리한 정문을 보아라
한 사람이 들어가기에는
너무 크게 열려 있고
다른 사람들에게는
언제나 닫혀 있다

열기 위해서가 아니라
닫기 위해서 있는
드나들기 위해서가 아니라
가로막기 위해서 있는
저것은 우리에게
문이 아니라
벽이다
우리를 가로막는
저 벽을

The new door

So that one single person
can go in and out about once a year
they have set up this enormous doorway
slap in the middle
with a dozen men guarding it day and night.
Keep Out.
Only look at that tremendous doorway
that ordinary people
may not use,
gaping wide open for just one man
to go in by,
and always closed
to everyone else.

That's not made to be opened,
it's made to be shut;
that's not made to be gone through,
it's made to be blocked.
That's not a door
for us,
it's a wall
so let's smash down
that wall

허물어뜨리자

아무도 밟지 못하게 하는
저 대리석 계단을
없애 버리자
아무도 가까이 갈 수 없는
저 화강암 기둥을
뽑아 버리자
아무도 드나들 수 없는
저 육중한 쇠문을
부숴 버리자

그리하여 없애 버리자
우리가 사용할 수 없는
저 큰 문을
없애 버리고 차라리
거기에다 벽을
만들자
그리고 그 벽에다
새로 문을
만들자
누구나 드나들 수 있는
그런 문을 만들자

blocking our way.

Let's destroy
those marble stairs
no one is permitted to tread on.
Let's uproot
those granite pillars
nobody is allowed to approach.
Let's break down
that iron gate
none can enter and leave by.

Yes, let's destroy them
and after destroying
that great door
no one can use,
instead let's build
a wall
and in that wall
let's build a new door.
let's build a door
everyone can
go in and out by.

O씨의 직업

우리 동네 O씨는
직업이 무엇일까

집 앞에 유달리 환한
방범등이 달려 있을 뿐
출퇴근이 분명치 않고
길에서 만날 수도 없어
그의 신분을 알 수 없었다
어느 날 그러나 동네 입구에
〈O喪家〉라는 화살표가 나붙자
좁은 골목 가득히 검은색
관용차들이 몰려들었다
눈빛 날카로운 인물을 한 명씩 태운
고급 승용차들이 사흘 동안 꼬리를 물고
왔다가
곧 되돌아갔다
택시를 타고 오거나 걸어서
문상오는 사람은 없었다

아 이제야 알겠다
O씨의 직업이 무엇인지를

Mr. O's Job

I often wondered what could be the job
of our neighbor Mr. O.

It's just that in front of his house
there was an unusually bright street light;
he kept no clear working hours
and since you never met him in the road,
there was no way of knowing his position.
Then one day down at the corner a sign appeared,
indicating someone in Mr. O's house had died
and at once black official cars began driving up,
filling the narrow roadway, and for several days
a succession of expensive cars,
each bearing a single needle-eyed passenger,
kept arriving
then soon leaving again
while there was no one who came by taxi
or on foot to offer condolence.

So now at last I know
what Mr. O's job is.

나무처럼 젊은이들도

동지달에도 날씨가 며칠 푸근하면
철없는 개나리는 노란 얼굴 내민다
봄이 오면 꽃샘추위 아랑곳없이
진달래는 곳곳에 소담스럽게 피어난다
피어나는 꽃의 마음을
가냘프다고
억누를 수 있느냐
어두운 땅 속으로 뻗어나가는 뿌리의 힘을
보이지 않는다고
업신여길 수 있느냐
땅에 깊숙이 뿌리 내리고
하늘로 피어오르는 꿈을
드높은 가지 끝에 품은
나무처럼 젊은이들도
힘차게 위로 솟아오르고
조용히 아래로 깊어지며
밝고 넓게 퍼져 나가기를
그러나 행여 잊지 말기를
아무리 높다란 나뭇가지 끝에서
저 들판 너머를 볼 수 있어도
뿌리는 언제나 땅 속에 있고
지하수가 수액이 되어

Young people like trees

Even in midwinter
if we have a few days of mild weather
the careless forsythia peeks out yellow cheeks.
When spring comes
azaleas burst into full bloom everywhere,
heedless of late frosts. Will anyone say
a blossoming flower's heart is fragile
and repress it? Can anyone say
that the power of the roots plunging deep
into the dark ground is invisible and despise it?
So with your roots plunged deep in the ground
and bearing dreams blossoming skywards
at the tips of your highest branches,
may you young people like trees—
springing up vigorously
pushing down quietly—
spread bright and wide.
But do not by some chance forget
that even when from the topmost tip of a lofty branch
can be glimpsed the far side of the plains,
unless the roots remain fixed in the ground
and spring water transformed into sap

남모르게 줄기 속을 흐르지 않으면
바람결에 멀리 향냄새 풍기는
아카시아도 라일락도
절대로 피어날 수 없음을

flows secretly inside the trunk,

neither the acacia nor the lilac,

whose perfume drifts from afar on the wind,

would ever be able to bloom.

젊은 손수운전자에게

네가 벌써 자동차를 갖게 되었으니
친구들이 부러워할 만도 하다
운전을 배울 때는
어디든지 달려갈 수 있을
네가 대견스러웠다
면허증은 무엇이나 따두는 것이
좋다고 나도 여러 번 말했었지
이제 너는 차를 몰고 달려가는구나
철따라 달라지는 가로수를 보지 못하고
길가의 과일 장수나 생선 장수를 보지 못하고
아픈 애기를 업고 뛰어가는 여인을 보지 못하고
교통 순경과 신호등을 살피면서
앞만 보고 달려가는구나
너의 눈은 빨라지고
너의 마음은 더욱 바빠졌다
앞으로 기름값이 또 오르고
매연이 눈앞을 가려도
너는 차를 두고
걸어다니려 하지 않을 테지
걷거나 뛰고
버스나 지하철을 타고 다니며
남들이 보내는 젊은 나이를 너는

To a young owner-driver

So you're already driving your own car?
I'll bet your friends are jealous!
As you were learning to drive,
I thought how splendid for you
to go speeding everywhere.
Getting any kind of license is good, I often said.
Now that you speed about in your car
you can't see the roadside trees changing with the seasons,
you can't see the merchants selling fruit
or fish at the roadside,
you can't see the woman running along
with a sick child slung on her back.
Always on the look-out for traffic-patrols and red lights,
your eyes fixed straight ahead, you speed about.
Your eyes have grown sharper,
your mind has grown busier,
and though the price of fuel may go up even more
and exhaust fumes block your view, you drive around
and do not intend to walk anywhere I'm sure.
You are spending at over 40 mph
those years of youth that other people spend
walking or running,

시속 60km 이상으로 지나가고 있구나
네가 차를 몰고 달려가는 것을 보면
너무 가볍게 멀어져 가는 것 같아
나의 마음이 무거워진다

getting about by bus or subway.

When I see you speeding along in your car

I feel you have isolated yourself too lightly

and my heart grows heavy.

봄 길

한 달에 한 번씩
아버지 따라
돌우물 할머니 산소에
성묘가던 길

봄 가뭄에
진흙먼지 날리는
삼십리 길을
고무신 신고
타박타박 걷노라면
그림자 밟힐 때쯤
풀무골에 닿았지

소달구지 지나가는
객주집 마루에 걸터앉아
잠깐 다리를 쉬며
아버지는 막걸리를 들고
나는 감주를 마셨지

길섶의 종달새
포르륵 머리 스치며
아지랑이처럼 나른한

Springtime road

Once every month,
I went following behind my father
on our way to pay our respects
at the tomb of Stonewell Village grandma.

Walking flip-flop
in white rubber shoes
along that four-mile path
with the dusty dried mud flying up
in the springtime drought,
we would arrive at Bellows Valley
about the time we were treading on our shadows.

Sprawled on the floor at the Peddler's Inn,
resting our legs a moment
while the oxcarts rumbled past,
father would drink makkoli
and I would sip rice syrup.

That spot where roadside larks
whirred skimming over our heads,
singing a weary drowsiness

졸음을 노래하던 곳

꼬리물고 떠오르는
온갖 기억 덧없어
오늘은 가족과 함께
자동차를 타고 달려가는
아스팔트길

like heat-haze shimmering—

all these memories
come rushing back in vain
as today with the whole family
we go speeding in our car
along an asphalted road.

Note: Makkolli is a milky, lightly alcoholic drink made using rice. It was drunk
during work to provide energy.

心電圖

가을 바람을 타고
잠자리들 날아오른다
나뭇잎들 떨어져도
돌아갈 곳 없는
텃새들의 자지러진 울음 소리
서리가 내리고
날이 일찍 저문다
눈발이 흩날릴 때쯤
철새들의 노래도 그치고
겨울 산은 한밤이 되어
어둡다 답답하다
땅은 깊이 잠들어
해가 떠도 깨어나지 않는다

텃새들의 수다스런 지저귐이
다시 꽃을 피우면
산비둘기 울 때마다
마을이 조금씩 밝아지고
뻐꾸기와 꾀꼬리 노래할 때는
산이 온통 환해진다
쓰르라미와 풀벌레 소리
물처럼 쏟아지는

Electrocardiogram

Borne on the autumn breeze

the dragonflies go soaring high.

Though the leaves fall,

the resident birds have nowhere to go

and their songs become bitter.

The frosts come

and the days end early.

Just as the first snowflakes come fluttering,

the calls of the passing migrant birds fall silent

and the winter hills become deep midnight,

dark and somber.

The earth falls fast asleep

and though the sun appears, it does not wake up.

When the busy chatter of the local birds

charms the flowers to bloom again

and every time the turtledoves coo

the village grows a little brighter.

When the cuckoo and the warbler call,

the mountains grow all radiant

and when it becomes high summer

with the songs of cicadas and insects

여름 날 한낮이 되면
나무들의 힘찬 맥박에
땅이 두근거리고
가물거리는 기억 속으로
어제 본 나비가 날아온다

pouring out like streams

to the strong pulse of the trees,

the earth too throbs

and in my flickering memory

a butterfly I saw yesterday comes fluttering by.

하얀 비둘기

애초에 비둘기를 기를 생각은 전혀 없었다.

다만 비오는 날 떼지어 날아다니는 비둘기가 몹시 축축하게 보여서, 구멍이 네 개 달린 비둘기집을 만들어 예쁘게 페인트 칠을 한 다음, 옥상 창문 위에 달아주었을 뿐이다.

그러나 사람의 마음 아랑곳없이 비둘기는 한 마리도 이곳에 날아들지 않았다.

십 년이 지나도록 마찬가지였다.

그 동안 비바람에 시달려 비둘기집은 칠이 벗겨지고 나무가 썩어서 보기 흉하게 되었다. 차라리 떼어버리는 것이 나을 듯싶었다.

그런데 며칠 전에 마당을 쓸다가 보니 하얀 비둘기 두 마리가 그 속에 앉아 있지 않은가.

우리 비둘기집은 다 낡아버린 뒤에야 비로소 비둘기의 마음에 들었나보다.

비둘기의 그 조그만 가슴속에 다른 하늘과 다른 땅이 있고, 그 가는 핏줄 속에 다른 물이 흐르고 다른 바람이 불고 있음을 나는 십 년 동안이나 몰랐던 셈이다.

White pigeons

Originally, I had no intention of raising pigeons.

But then one rainy day the flocks of pigeons flying about looked so miserably damp, that I made a nesting box with four holes, painted it nicely, then fixed it above the attic window, nothing more.

Yet despite my humane concern, not one single pigeon came flying in that direction.

Ten years passed, and it was still the same.

Meanwhile, wind and rain had left the nesting box stripped of its paint, the wood was rotten, it was a disgrace to look at. I reckoned I'd do better to take it down.

Yet just a few days ago, looking up as I was sweeping the yard, I realized that two white pigeons were ensconced inside it.

It seems that our nesting box could only make a pigeon's heart happy once it was old and decayed.

It took me ten years to realize that there are a different heaven and a different earth within a pigeon's tiny breast, that another fluid flows in its veins, another wind blows there.

잠자리

늦가을 엷은 햇살
빨랫줄 위에
꽁지를 약간 치켜들고
잠자리 한 마리

커다란 눈
가느다란 목
비치는 날개

가볍게 하르르 날다가
감나무 가지 끝에
사뿐히 옮겨 앉는다

바람도 잠시 숨죽이고
모든 눈길이 자기에게 쏠려도
잠자리는 외치지 않는다
눈물 흘리지 않고
노래 부르지 않는다

꼼짝도 하지 않고
무게도 없이
그저 제자리에
머물러 있을 뿐

Dragonfly

In the weak sunlight of late autumn
a single dragonfly perches
on the washing line
its head slightly raised

huge eyes
slender neck
transparent wings.

Whirring lightly up,
gently it transfers its perch
to the tip of a persimmon tree branch.

Though the breeze briefly drops
and all eyes are fixed on it
the dragonfly does not call out.
It does not weep
and does not sing.

It does not budge, either,
but simply stays
where it is,
weightless.

나뭇잎 하나

크낙산 골짜기가 온통
연록색으로 부풀어올랐을 때
그러니까 신록이 우거졌을 때
그곳을 지나가면서 나는
미처 몰랐었다

뒷절로 가는 길이 온통
주황색 단풍으로 물들고 나뭇잎들
무더기로 바람에 떨어지던 때
그러니까 낙엽이 지던 때도
그곳을 거닐면서 나는
느끼지 못했었다

이렇게 한 해가 다 가고
눈발이 드문드문 흩날리던 날
앙상한 대추나무 가지 끝에 매달려 있던
나뭇잎 하나
문득 혼자서 떨어졌다

저마다 한 개씩 돋아나
여럿이 모여서 한여름 살고
마침내 저마다 한 개씩 떨어져

One leaf

When the valley in Keunaksan Mountain was all
buoyant with pale green,
when the trees were thick with fresh leaves, I mean,
I had no idea at all
as I passed by.

When the road to the temple beyond was
all ablaze with orange maples and leaves
were falling in mounds in the breeze
when the dead leaves were falling, I mean,
I did not feel anything at all
as I strolled by.

One day when the year was virtually over
and occasional snowflakes fluttered down,
one leaf
dangling at the tip of a branch of a gaunt jujube tree
suddenly fell, all alone.

Each of them had sprouted separately,
lived through the summer clustered together
then finally each had fallen separately

그 많은 나뭇잎들
사라지는 것을 보여주면서

and as they did so, each of those leaves

was showing what it is to vanish.

가을날

누가 부는지 뒷산에서
서투른 나팔 소리 들려온다
견딜 수 없는 피로 때문에
끝내 약속을 지키지 못했다는
그의 말이 문득 떠오른다
여름내 햇볕 즐기며
윤나는 잎사귀 반짝이던 감나무에
지금은 까치밥 몇 개
높다랗게 매달려 있고
땅에는 떨어진 열매들
아무도 줍지 않았다
나는 어디쯤 떨어질 것인가
낯익은 골목길 모퉁이
어느 공원 벤치에도 이제는
기다릴 사람 없다
차라리 늦가을 벌레 소리에 묻혀
지난날의 꿈을 꾸고
꿈 속에서 깨어나
손짓하는 코스모스에게 묻고 싶다
봄에는 너를 보지 못했다
여름에는 어디 있었니
때늦게 길가에 피어난 꽃들

An autumn day

I don't know who's playing but I can hear the sound
of a trumpet played badly on the hill behind our house.
Abruptly I recall his words, when he said
that because of an overwhelming fatigue
he had finally not been able to keep his promise.
On the persimmon tree, where lustrous leaves
sparkled all summer long,
now only a few persimmons remain
hanging high up to feed the birds
while no one has picked up
others, that have fallen to the ground.
I wonder where I shall fall.
There is no one for me to wait for now
at the corner of a familiar alley
or on some bench in a park.
Immersed in the songs of late-autumn insects
I dream dreams of bygone days
then waking from those dreams
I long to question the waving cosmos flowers:
I could not see you in springtime.
Where were you all summer long?
Flowers blooming so late along the roadsides,

함초롬히 입 가리고 웃을 것이다
아직도 누군가 만나
나누고 싶은 이야기
굳게 입 다물고
두꺼운 안경으로 눈 가리고
앓고 싶지 않은 병
온몸에 간직한 채 나는
아무렇지도 않은 듯
천천히 그곳으로 다가가고 있다
아득한 젊은 날을 되풀이하는
서투른 나팔 소리
참을 수 없는 졸음 때문에
마지막 기회를 잃어버렸다는
그의 말을 이제는 알 것 같다

you laugh delightfully, modestly hiding your mouths.

Still I want to meet someone

and share talk with them

but with lips tightly shut,

eyes hidden behind thick glasses,

and a disease I do not want to suffer from

buried deep within me,

I am heading slowly toward that same place,

pretending it does not matter at all.

The sound of a trumpet being played badly

recalls far off days of youth—

because of an overwhelming fatigue

I have missed my last chance,

is what he said and now I think I understand.

나무

봄이 와도 당신은 꽃씨를 뿌리지 않는다. 어린 나무를 옮겨 심지 않는다.

철 따라 물을 주고, 살충제를 뿌리고, 가지를 쳐주고, 밑동을 싸맬 필요도 없다.

이미 커다랗게 자란 장미, 목련, 무궁화, 화양목, 주목, 벽오동, 산수유, 영산홍, 청단풍, 등나무, 모과나무, 앵두나무, 감나무, 대추나무, 살구나무, 잣나무, 은행나무, 가이즈카향나무, 겹벚나무, 사철나무, 자귀나무, 대나무, 플라타너스, 느티나무, 소나무, 눈향나무, 박태기나무 들을 사들이면 되기 때문이다.

거대한 정원을 가득 채운 저 수많은 관상수들을 당신은 모두 나무라고 부른다.

당신은 참으로 많은 나무를 가지고 있다. 단 한 그루의 나무 이름조차 모르면서도.

Trees

Even though spring has come, you sow no flower seeds. You transplant no seedling trees.

You do not need to water, sprinkle insecticide, prune, wrap up trunks.

All you have to do is purchase fully grown roses, magnolias, rose-of-Sharon, box, yew, parasol trees, hawthorn, rhododendron, maple, wisteria, quince, wild plum trees, persimmon, jujube, apricot, pine trees, gingko trees, juniper, cherry trees, spindle trees, silk trees, bamboo, plane trees, zelkova trees, firs, Judas trees.

And all those ornamental trees filling your vast estate — you simply call them "trees."

You own a tremendous number of trees. Yet you don't know the name of even one.

나사에 관하여

창고마다 지저분하게 널려진
수백만 개의 나사들
크기만 다를 뿐 모두 비슷한
암나사와 숫나사들을
한 번도 눈여겨본 적이 없다
도무지 매력 없어 보이는 저것들이
수많은 부품을 합치고 조이면
자동차가 되어 달려가고
비행기가 되어 날아가고
로보트가 되어 작동한다
는 것을 알고는 있었다
어쩌다 한 개의 숫나사가 빠지거나
한 개의 암나사가 부서지면
그 한 개의 나사 때문에
자동차의 엔진이 꺼지고
비행기가 불시착하고
로보트가 작동하지 않는다
는 것을 알고는 있었다
그러나 한 개의 나사 때문에
귀중한 목숨을 잃기 전에
그리고 한 개의 나사를 갈아끼우기 위하여
수천 개의 나사를 풀어야 하기 전에

About screws

I have never once observed properly
the millions of screws
lying scattered in disorder in every warehouse—
female nuts and male bolts
all alike except for their size.
Completely devoid of charm, they
join together a host of spare parts when tightened—
form a car and speed away,
form a plane and fly away,
form a robot and move about—
that much I knew.
Yet if a single screw falls out
or a single nut breaks,
on account of a single screw
a car's engine stops running
a plane makes a forced landing
a robot stops moving—
that too I knew.
But before one precious life is lost
on account of a single screw,
have you never thought
what has to be done and how

무엇을 어떻게 해야 할 것인지
한 번도 생각해본 적이 없느냐

before undoing thousands of bolts

in order to replace one screw

당신들의 용병

배불리 먹고
늘어지게 자고
비디오를 보거나
실내 수영을 즐기고
참으로 따분한 생활이다
30년이 훨씬 지나도록 이 땅에는
전쟁이 없었다
무료한 안정과 평화
이제는 지긋지긋하다
차라리 외인부대 병사처럼
웃통 벗어 젖히고
가관단총 난사하면서
적진으로 달려 들어가
피를 뿜으며
거꾸러지고 싶다
대기업 신입사원으로 들어가
갑종근로소득세 꼬박꼬박 내면서
지루하게 일생을 살아가느니
차라리 도시 게릴라처럼
명망가의 등을 칼로 찌르고
재벌의 딸을 납치하고
주유소에 불을 지르고

Your tactics

Eating your fill,
sleeping as long as you want,
watching videos,
enjoying an indoor swim—
such a tedious life.
For well over thirty years now
the country has known no war.
Security and peace free of charge
have by now grown wearisome.
I want to go racing toward the enemy lines
stripped to the waist, head thrown back,
firing a submachine-gun wildly
then collapse in a shower of blood.
Starting work as a new employee in a big company
regularly paying income tax
and living a boring life,
I want to stab distinguished citizens in the back
like some urban guerrilla
kidnap the daughters of top businessmen
set fire to gas stations
be pursued by police and MPs
and dive into the Han River.

경찰과 헌병에게 쫓기다가
한강으로 뛰어내리고 싶다
아무것도 바라지 않는
이 순수한 욕망
당신들은 모를 것이다
서울빌딩 주차장의 붉은 낙서를
누가 썼는지
끝내 모를 것이다
땡볕 아래 엎드려 온종일
논밭을 매는 당신들이여
졸음을 참아가면서 밤새워
기계를 돌리는 당신들이여
온종일 개혁 정책을 연구하고
밤새워 혁명 전략을 토론하는
당신들이여

All of you will know nothing

of this pure desire

completely without expectations.

You'll never know

who wrote that red inscription

in the car park of Seoul Building.

All you who work bent over all day long

weeding the rice-paddies and fields,

all you who keep machines turning   ·

all night long, fighting off sleep,

all you

who spend all day studying reform policies

and all night discussing revolutionary strategies . . . .

작은 꽃들

사방에서 터져 올라간 최루탄 가스
마침내 하늘의 코를 찔렀나보다
때아닌 태풍에 비바람 휘몰아쳐
탐스런 목련꽃들 모조리 떨어뜨리고
새로 심은 가로수 뿌리째 뽑아놓고
서울빌딩 간판까지 날려버렸다
갓 피어난 작은 꽃들 애처롭게
몽땅 떨어졌을 줄 알았는데
철늦은 꽃샘바람 지나간 뒤
길가의 개나리 눈부시게 노랗고
언덕 위의 진달래 활짝 피었다
빗속에 떨던 조그만 꽃이파리들
바람에 시달리던 가녀린 꽃줄기들
떨어져나간 간판 버팀쇠보다
오히려 굳세게 봄을 지키고 있구나

Little flowers

It looked as if the tear-gas being fired off in all directions
had finally tickled the sky's nose.
In an unseasonable typhoon, wind and rain did their worst
so that all the delicate magnolia flowers drooped,
newly planted roadside trees were uprooted
and the signboards on Seoul Building went flying off.
I fully expected that all the little flowers in bloom
would fall in great masses
but once the belated cold wind was over
the forsythias along the roadsides were still dazzling yellow
and azaleas were in full bloom across the hillsides.
The petals of the little flowers that trembled in the rain,
the delicate stalks that had been tossed in the storm
remained more stoutly faithful to springtime
than the steel supports of fallen signboards.

떠나기

아무도 오라고 하지 않고
가라고 하지 않을 때
처음으로 나는 혼자서 떠났다
오랫동안 정든 곳을 떠나
낯선 곳에 머물다가
처음으로 나는 돌아왔다
반갑게 맞아주고
따뜻하게 보살펴주어
편안히 한동안 머물다가
나는 다시 떠났다
모두들 말리면서
못 가게 했지만
고집스럽게 뿌리치고
다시 떠났다
어느 곳이든 가서
머물다가
익숙해질 때쯤
그곳을 떠났다
때로는 붙잡고
못 떠나게 해서
차라리 그대로 머물까 망설이다가
기어코 또 떠났다

Leaving

There was no one asking me to come
no one telling me to go, when
for the first time I left, all alone.
Leaving a place I had long grown fond of,
after staying awhile in an unfamiliar place
for the first time I came back.
Welcomed joyfully,
tended warmly,
I stayed there peacefully for a time
then I left again.
Everyone urged me not to,
tried to prevent me from going
but stubbornly pulling up my roots
I left again.
Going nowhere in particular,
staying awhile,
when I had grown used to it
I would leave that place.
Sometimes people caught hold of me
prevented me from leaving
so I would hesitate whether to stay or not
then finally leave.

한곳에 오래 머물지 않고
끊임없이 떠나고
다시 돌아왔다
즐거운 집 사랑스런 가족을 두고
이제 또 떠나야겠다
다시 돌아올 수 없을지라도

Not staying in any one place for long

endlessly leaving

I would then come back again.

Turning my back on a happy household, loving family,

I shall soon be having to leave again.

Though I may never be able to come back again.

그들의 승리

그들은 원래 소수파였다.

그러나 결코 가만히 있지 않았다.

언제나 몰려다니며 잘못을 캐내고 밤낮으로 토론하여 유리한 구실을 찾아냈다. 자기들은 항상 정당하고 남들은 항상 부당했다.

그들은 끊임없이 주장하고 요구하고 도전했다.

무엇이든지 물어뜯고 흔들어대고 떠벌였다. 누구든지 한번 그들에게 잡히면 달아나려고 해도 놓아주지 않았다.

힘이 모자라도 절대로 물러서지 않았다. 욕설을 퍼부며 덤벼들어 할퀴고 딴죽을 걸거나 뒤에서 돌팔매질을 했다.

한마디로 그들은 상종할 수 없는 무리였다.

모두들 그들을 피했다.

다수파조차도 그들과 대결하려 들지 않았다. 그들과 싸우느니 차라리 이쪽에서 미리 두 손을 드는 것이 낫다고 생각했다. 하지만 그들은 항복도 받아들이지 않았다.

그리하여 모두 스스로 목숨을 끊었고, 세상에는 결국 그들만 남게 되었다.

Their victory

Originally they were only a small minority.

But they refused to keep quiet.

All the time pursued, they revealed errors, held discussions day and night, and so obtained lucrative positions. They were always in the right, others always in the wrong.

They endlessly asserted, demanded, challenged.

They bit, shook, exaggerated everything. If someone once fell into their hands they would never let go, no matter how hard they tried to escape.

Even if their power was insufficient, they would never back off. Uttering curses they would attack, claw, trip, and throw stones from behind.

In a word they were a mob you could not associate with.

Everyone avoided them.

Even the majority avoided a showdown with them. Better to hold up both hands first, rather that fight with them, they reckoned. But they accepted no surrender.

Finally, everyone else put an end to their life, so that only they were left in the world.

돌 옷

그 행위 예술가는 일찍이 한강대교를 몽땅 비닐로 싸매려고 시도해서 세상을 놀라게 한 바 있었다.

인왕산의 헌칠한 미끄럼바위에도 언젠가 거대한 의상을 입히겠다고 공언했었다.

당국의 허가를 얻어 그 꿈을 미처 펼치기도 전에, 그가 교통 사고로 타계한 것은 참으로 애석한 일이다.

하지만 아직도 그가 살아 있다면,

놀랄 것이다. 아무 말 없이 그 커다란 바위가 자디잔 이끼와 담쟁이덩굴로 연녹색 여름옷을 해 입은 것을 보고.

Dressed stone

That action artist once amazed the world with his plan to wrap the entire main bridge over the Han River in plastic.

He also declared that one day he would dress the elegant smooth rock on Mount Inwang in a gigantic suit of clothes.

It is truly regrettable that he departed this life in a traffic accident before he could get the authorities' permission and realize his dream.

But if he were still alive,

he would be amazed. Without so much as a word, that huge rock has donned summer clothes of pale green, made from the finest moss and creeping ivy.

Note: Mount Inwang. This hill, the upper parts of which are mainly naked walls of granite, lies to the west of the royal palaces in central Seoul. Kim Kwang-Kyu was born, grew up and still lives at the foot of this hill.

오솔길

지장보살 앞에 놓인
亡者들의 사진
내 또래도 눈에 띄고
젊은 얼굴도 더러 있다
나도 꽤 오래 살았구나
손주의 운동화 빌려 신고
절을 찾아온 할머니들과
중년 등산객들 틈에 끼어 서서
冥府殿을 기웃거린다
어둑한 침묵의 한 구석에
목탁과 福田函
주민등록증과 돈지갑이 들어 있는
바른쪽 속주머니를 지나
갈빗대 밑에서
뜨끔거리며 자라는 죽음
어버이를 잃거나
자식을 낳거나
먹고 마시고 즐기며
五十年을 어질러놓은 자리
서둘러 대충대충 치우려 해도
이제는 빠듯한 시간이다
아무도 눈치채지 못하게

The narrow path

Among the photos of dead people
arranged before the image of Ksitigarbha Bodhisattva
those of people my age strike my eye
though there are younger faces as well.
Hey, I've lived a really long life!
Standing there wedged among old women
who have borrowed their grandchildren's sneakers
to climb up to the temple,
and middle-aged hikers
I peer at the Court of the World Beyond.
In one corner of the dimly lit stillness I see
a wooden gong and a box for offerings.
Below my right-hand inside pocket
holding my wallet and ID card
underneath my rib-cage
death tingles and grows.
We lose parents,
have children
eat, drink, enjoy ourselves
scattering fifty years about
and when we quickly try to put things in order
we find that time is limited now.

슬픔의 배낭 조금씩 줄이고
그림자 슬며시 숲속에 남겨두고
일찍 어둡는 산길
혼자서 총총히
떠나야겠구나

Carefully, so no one notices,

we bit by bit reduce the backpack of sorrow

furtively abandon shadows in the woods

for we'll have to set off hurriedly

down the early darkening mountain path alone.

Note: The Court of the World Beyond. In many Buddhist temples, one hall contains a representation of the group of immortals who are thought to pass judgment on the souls of those who die, dispatching those who have deserved it to various forms of infernal punishment from which they may be saved by Ksitigarbha Bodhisattva. Such halls are used for rituals and chanting designed to assist the dead, whose photos are often enshrined there.

있다는 것

그는 흙으로 돌아갔다
돌아간다는 것
하루 일을 끝내고
집으로 돌아간다는 것
자식들이 속을 썩이고
마누라가 바가지를 긁어도
집으로 돌아올 수 있다는 것
별다른 희망이 없더라도
신문을 뒤적거리고
창 밖의 전신주를 바라보거나
책상서랍을 정리할 수 있다는 것
밀린 편지를 쓸 수 있다는 것
고단한 몸을 눕혔다가
아침에 다시 일어날 수 있다는 것
다행스럽게도 이렇게 살고 있다는 것이
슬퍼졌다
친구의 장례를 치르고
돌아온 다음부터
나는 눈이 여려졌다

Being

He's gone back to being dust.
Going back.
After finishing the day's work,
going back home . . .
The fact of being able to come back home
even though the children are troublesome
and the wife nags.
Even if there's no great hope of anything changing,
being able to browse through the newspaper,
stare through the window at a telegraph pole
or clear out a drawer in your desk.
Being able to write a belated letter.
Being able to throw your weary body down
and get up again the next morning.
Being luckily able to live like this
has grown sad.
Ever since I came back
from attending a friend's funeral
my eyes have grown sensitive.

五友歌

바위와 나무가 가려주었지
우리가 처음으로 사랑을 나누던 때
닫혀진 스틸도어나 내려진 커튼이 아니라
널려진 바윗돌과 대나뭇잎들이 우리를 감추어주었지

소나무 숲속에 엎드려 숨죽이던 때
끈질기게 뒤쫓는 그들로부터 우리를 지켜준 것은
수류탄이나 기관총이 아니라
귀가 멍멍하게 쏟아져내리는 폭포 소리였지

북두칠성을 뒤돌아보면서
굶주린 발길을 海南으로 재촉하던 때
어둠 속에서 우리를 이끌어준 것은
강철 같은 이념이 아니라 희미한 달빛이었지

Song for five friends

Rocks and trees formed a screen.

When we first shared love, we were concealed,

not by closed steel doors or drawn curtains

but by scattered stones and bamboo leaves.

When we lay holding our breath in the pine forest,

what sheltered us from those tenacious pursuers

was not grenades or machine guns

but the deafening sound of a waterfall pouring down.

When we hastened southward with starving steps,

all the time looking back at the seven stars of the Great Bear,

what guided us through the darkness

was not some iron-hard ideology but the faint moonlight.

Note: This poem is inspired by a famous lyric by the scholar-poet Yun Seon-do
(1587–1671) that many generations of Korean schoolchildren have memorized.
The old poem is a celebration of the beauties of nature in six four-line stanzas,
showing the poet withdrawing from human society. The present poem echoes the
images of nature found in Yun's poem, but from a very different perspective,
evoking the horrors of the Korean War.

한 사람 또는 몇 사람이

젊은이들 모두 떠나가버린 들녘에서
늙은 농부 한 사람이
메마른 논에 물을 대고 있다

바캉스를 즐기려 산으로 바다로 달려가는 한여름
불볕 내리쬐는 고속도로 분리대 주변에서
수건을 쓴 청소원 몇 사람이
쓰레기를 줍고 있다

노학연계투쟁이 한바탕 지나간 학생회관 앞마당
나뒹구는 화염병 유리 조각 최루탄 파편 유인물 전단
관리과 잡역부 몇 사람이
힘겹게 치우고 있다

앞장서 투쟁하던 간부들 코를 고는 겨울 밤
창고 옆 숙직실에서 라면을 끓이며
나이 어린 공원 한 사람이
다친 동료를 돌보고 있다

누군가 한 사람 또는 몇 사람이
흔들리는 기둥을 붙들고 있어 그래도
이 세상이 무너지지 않는다

One or a few

Out in the plains that the young have all abandoned
one elderly farmer
is irrigating a parched paddy field.

Near an intersection in the midsummer motorway, sunlight
beating down, where people are speeding off to enjoy holidays
in the hills or by the sea, a few sweepers, heads wrapped in
towels, are picking up litter.

In front of the student union, where a student demonstration
in support of workers has just ended, a few university
employees are laboriously clearing up the scattered glass of
fire-bombs, splinters of tear-gas grenades, pamphlets.

On a winter's night the leaders of the workers' struggle are
snoring in the night-watchman's shed beside the warehouse,
while one young machinist cooking instant noodles tends to a
wounded comrade.

So long as somebody, one or a few,
is holding up the tottering pillars, at least
this world will not collapse.

까치의 고향

아침 까치 짖는 소리
뒤꼍 장독대를 울린다
반가운 손님 찾아올 징조는 옛말
낡은 기와지붕 아래 이제는
떠나야 할 사람뿐이다
앞마당에 잡초 가득 퍼지고
주저앉은 헛간에 녹슨 경운기
무엇을 더 기다리겠나
강아지 밥그릇에 말라붙은
까만 콩 두 개
내려다보고 감나무 가지에서
꽁지 흔들며 짖어대는
까치 한 마리뿐이다

Magpies back home

The sound of magpies squawking in the early morning

rings over the storage platform in the back yard—

a sign that welcome visitors will be coming,

an old saying claims

but nowadays all there is under the ancient tiled roof

is one person who'll soon be obliged to leave.

The front yard is overgrown with weeds,

in the tumble-down shed a rusty cultivator—

what would be the point of waiting any longer?

Looking down at the two black beans

stuck dried to the dog's feeding bowl,

wagging its tail and squawking from a branch

in the persimmon tree, one solitary magpie, that's all . . .

노루목 밭터

봉구네 집이 헐값에 팔고 떠난
노루목 밭터에 언제부턴가
시퍼런 드럼통과 시뻘건 양철 박스
하나둘 뒹굴더니
옛날 노적가리보다 훨씬 높게 쌓여
사방에 응달을 펼치고
고약한 냄새 풍겨
까마귀조차 내려앉지 않는다
양조장집에서 공장터로 사들인
사슴배미 논자리도 언제부턴가
부서진 자동차 뼈다귀와 못쓰는 타이어
고장난 냉장고와 가스 레인지
엔진 오일 찌꺼기와 깨어진 유리 조각들로
발 디딜 수 없는 쓰레기터 되었고
동네 우물물에서 석유맛 난다
한밤에도 메밀꽃 환하던 밭터
여름에는 우렁을 건지던 논배미
두엄 썩는 마당에 쇠방울 소리
이제는 모두 TV 화면 속으로 사라졌다

The field at Deer's Neck

For some time now the field at Deer's Neck
that Pong-gu's family sold for a song before they left
has been piled here and there
with blue oil-drums and red metal boxes—
rising much higher than the grain stacks in the old days—
casting their shade in all directions and emitting such a foul
stench that not even magpies stop there.
Stag's Piece paddy-field, purchased by a beer company
to build a brewery on, has for some time now
become a garbage dump
strewn with wrecked car bodies and unusable tires
broken refrigerators and gas stoves,
dregs of engine oil and broken glass,
so that no one can so much as set foot on it
and the local well-water tastes of kerosene.
That field once bright with buckwheat flowers even at midnight,
where we used to collect mud-snails in summer,
the sound of the cow-bell out in the yard with its rotting
manure—
nowadays all that has vanished into the TV screen.

殺母蛇

자기를 낳아
길러준
어미까지 잡아먹었으면
그래도 무엇인가 되었어야 한다
아직도 그저 한 마리의
뱀이란 말이냐
어미를 잡아먹는
새끼를 또 낳겠단 말이냐

Matricidal snakes

Even if you devoured the very mother

who bore you

and raised you,

you would still have to become something.

Perhaps simply

a snake—

destined to give birth in turn to baby snakes

that then eat their mother.

어느 選帝侯의 동상

한때 그는 이 나라를 다스리던 막강한 선제후였다.

지금도 시청 앞 광장 한가운데 아득히 높은 곳에서 그는 이 도시 전체를 한눈에 내려다보고 있다.

그의 동상을 올려다보면, 누구나 경탄을 금할 수 없다. 높이 135미터의 원주 위에 저 육중한 구리 덩어리를 올려 놓은 당시의 기술도 놀랍거니와, 그 오랜 세월을 비바람 속에서 의연하게 수직으로 서 있도록 만든 옛사람들의 솜씨 또한 뛰어나지 않은가.

저것은 그러나 역사의 가혹한 유물임에 틀림없다.

새들이 콧잔등에 똥을 깔겨도 눈 한번 깜빡거리지 못하고, 발이 저리고 겨드랑이가 가려워도 손가락 한 개 움직이지 못하고, 저 아슬아슬한 기둥 꼭대기에서 몇백 년을 현기증에 시달리고 있으니 말이다.

엄청난 재력과 부역을 동원하여 스스로의 형벌까지 마련해놓은 위대한 선제후여.

A great lord's bronze statue

Once he was a mighty lord who ruled over this nation.

Still today, he gazes down on this entire city from a vast height, directly in front of City Hall.

No one can help being impressed on climbing up to his bronze statue. The technology of that era, capable of raising that ponderous mass of bronze on to the top of its 135-meter high column, astounds, and equally outstanding, surely is the skill of those long-ago people who made it capable of standing resolutely upright through all those long ages of wind and rain.

There is no doubt that that statue is a brutal legacy of history.

When birds shit on the ridge of his nose, he can't so much as blink; when his leg grows numb or his armpit itches, he can't budge a finger; and he's been subject to vertigo up on top of that dizzying column for centuries now.

You were a great lord, indeed, mobilizing such vast resources of wealth and slave-labor to prepare your own punishment.

바닥

낮게 드리운 구름
양떼들 한가롭게 풀 뜯는 초원
짙푸른 숲과 영롱한 새소리
뷔르바하 마을의 박공 지붕과 교회 첨탑
파란 눈의 노랑머리 아가씨들
모두가 내 고향과 다른데
산책길에 밟히는 민들레 질경이 억새풀
길바닥 잡초들은 똑같다
군데군데 드러난 땅바닥
진흙 색깔은 어디나 똑같다

Floor

Low-hanging clouds,

grasslands where sheep graze at leisure,

dark green woods and bright birdsong,

the gabled roofs and church tower of Burbach village,

the blue-eyed, yellow-haired girls—

all so different from my own home yet

the dandelions, plantains, rushes I tread along the path,

the plants forming the floor of the path, are just the same.

The color of the earth of the path floor,

glimpsed here and there is everywhere just the same.

Note: Burbach is a small village in the Siegerland region of Germany, where Kim Kwang-Kyu lived in 1991 while he was working as a visiting professor.

어둠 속 걷기

어둠이 내리기 시작하면, 그들은 눈을 비비며 깨어나는 모양이다. 그들 가운데는 내가 아는 얼굴도 많다.

장악원장 할아버지는 거실 안락의자에 앉아 근엄하게 수염을 쓰다듬고 있다. 누하동 할머니는 끊어진 전구를 양말 속에 넣고, 구멍 뚫린 뒤꿈치를 깁고 있다.

정치에서 손을 뗀 뒤부터, 아버지는 옛날 책력을 뒤적거리거나, 앞뜰 채마밭을 가꾸며 소일한다. 큰 항아리에서 바가지로 쌀을 떠내다가 갑자기 돌아가신 어머니는 아직도 광 문 앞에 쓰러져 있다. 누님은 큰절을 되풀이하며, 자꾸만 지장보살을 되뇌인다.

시역의 총탄에 맞아 피를 흘리는 김구 선생과 교수형을 당한 죽산의 데드 마스크도 보인다. 사일구 때 죽은 친구들이 여전히 젊은 모습으로 왔다갔다 하고, 분신 자살한 투사들은 중화상으로 괴로워하고 있다.

이처럼 한밤중에는 우리 집안이나 마당뿐만 아니라, 서울과 시골, 산과 들, 강과 바다가 온통 죽은 이들로 가득차 있어, 이들을 피하여 발걸음을 옮기기가 여간 힘들지 않다.

Walking in the dark

As night begins to fall, they rub their eyes as if just waking up. Among them are a lot of familiar faces.

My ancestor who was once Minister for Music is sitting in the armchair in his room, gravely stroking his beard. My Grandmother from Seoul's Nuha-dong is putting a burned-out light-bulb into a sock and darning the hole in the heel.

After retiring from politics, Father kills time leafing through old almanacs, or digging in the vegetable patch. Mother who died just as she was scooping rice out of the big crock is still lying as she fell before the door. Sister is making deep prostrations, invoking Ksitigarbha Bodhisattva.

Kim Ku still bleeds from the assassin's bullet, and I can see the death-mask of wrongfully executed Chuksan. Friends killed in the 1960 Revolution come and go, looking as young as ever, while protesters who set themselves alight still suffer from their burns.

At night it's like this, not only in our house and garden, in Seoul and in the countryside—mountains and fields, river and sea are all so full of the dead that it's hard to avoid them as you walk.

캄캄한 어둠 속을 걸어가기는 그래서 어려운 것이다.

That's why walking in the dark is so difficult.

Note: Kim Ku (1876–1949) was a noted Korean patriot and Independence fighter who was several times imprisoned during the Japanese colonial period(1910–1945). In 1944 he became president of the Provisional Korean Government in Exile in Shanghai. After Liberation, he strove to keep left- and right-wing forces together for the creation of an independent Korea. He was highly respected by many but was assassinated in the midst of the turmoil prior to the Korean war.

Chuksan is the 'Ho'(pen-name) of Cho Bong-am (1898–1959) who helped found the Communist Party of Korea as a means of opposing Japanese rule. Soon after Independence, he left the party and became a politician in South Korea, where he became the first Agriculture Minister of the Republic of Korea. In 1956, having failed to defeat the then president Syngman Rhee in elections, he founded a Progressive Party. This led to accusations of subversion and he was hanged as a pro-communist in the year before the April Revolution(1960).

물 길

언젠가 왔던 길을 누가
물보다 잘 기억하겠나
아무리 재주껏 가리고
깊숙이 숨겨놓아도
물은
어김없이 찾아와
자기의 몸을 담아보고
자기의 깊이를 주장하느니
여보게
억지로 막으려 하지 말게
제 가는 대로 꾸불꾸불 넓고 깊게
물길 터주면
고인 곳마다 시원하고
흐를 때는 아름다운 것을
물과 함께 아니라면 어떻게
먼 길을 갈 수 있겠나
누가 혼자 살 수 있겠나

Waterway

Will anyone ever manage better than water

to recall the way they came?

No matter how arduously you hide it

how deep you conceal it

water

unfailingly finds its way

fills itself up

asserts its own depths

so look,

don't try to block it by force.

If you leave a way open

for the waterways

to take their own course, broad and deep,

every place where they settle will be cool

and when they flow if that is not a beautiful place

with water, how will we be able to travel long distances ?

Can anyone live alone ?

화초의 가족

아파트로 이사온 뒤부터 화분을 줄이게 되었다.

지난해에는 선인장과 마령초가 바깥에서 겨울을 맞았다. 가을에 안으로 들여놓지 않으면, 화초는 밖에서 얼어 죽을 수밖에 없다.

올 가을에도 제라늄과 문주란이 안으로 들어오지 못했다. 오디오 시스템과 퍼스널 컴퓨터와 헬스 기구가 늘어나는 바람에, 화분을 들여놓을 자리가 줄어들었기 때문이다.

그래도 치자와 오죽, 벽오동과 감귤나무, 소철과 포인세티아는 좁은 거실을 가득 채우고, 저마다 품위를 자랑한다. 이것들은 이제 우리 아이들보다도 나이가 많다.

전자 제품과 인스턴트 식품만 좋아하는 아이들은 이 오래 된 화초들을 싫어한다. 가로거친다 흘겨보고, 내가 없으면 물도 주지 않는다.

내년 가을에는 어느 화초가 바깥에서 겨울을 맞게 될지. 누런 잎을 따주면서, 나는 차츰 화초의 가족이 되어 가고 있다.

Family with potted plants

When we moved to a new apartment, we reduced the number of our potted plants.

Last year a cactus and a tuber were left exposed to the winter outside. Unless we bring them inside during the winter, potted plants are certain to freeze to death.

This autumn too, I failed to bring in a geranium and a crinum. That was because, what with the audio system and the personal computer, and the health machine taking up more room, I was obliged to reduce the space for plants.

Nonetheless, a gardenia and a black bamboo, a phoenix tree and a tangerine bush, a sago palm and a poinsettia filled every inch of the small sitting room, each one boasting of its dignity. After all, they are older than our children by now.

The children love electronic gadgets and instant food; they detest these old potted plants. Edging past, they look at them askance, not watering them if I'm not around.

Which plant will be exposed to the winter outside next year ? As I nip off yellowing leaves, I am gradually becoming part of the family of potted plants.

나쁜 놈

화장을 짙게 하는 아내
요통이나 견비통으로 고생하는 동창생들
생명보험에 든 선배와 정년 퇴직한 스승
예수를 보았다는 어머니
모두 젖혀놓고
한마디의 다툼도 없이 그는
훌쩍 떠나갔다
지독한 냄새 풍기는
자기의 시체 앞에다
우리들 모두 엄숙한 얼굴로
무릎꿇게 하고
혼자서 훌쩍 가버렸다
아직도 오래 치욕스런 나날을 살아갈
그 많은 동시대인들에게
짓궂게 낄낄 웃는 사진 한 장
남겨놓은 채
포클레인이 잠깐 사이에 파놓은
흙구덩이 속에
묻혀버렸다
산과 들 온통 덮어주는
함박눈의 축하까지 받으면서

Bad guy

He left them all standing—

his wife with her heavy make-up

his old school friends with their lumbago or rheumatics

his older friends with their life insurance and his retired

teacher

his mother who claimed she had seen Jesus—

without a word of complaint, he simply left.

He made us all bend our knees

with serious faces

before his corpse

that was giving off a foul smell

and set off all alone.

Leaving behind a photo

in which he was grinning in a harassing way

at all his contemporaries

who were going to have to go on with their living hell,

he was buried

in a hole in the ground

dug in a flash by a mechanical digger,

even receiving good wishes from the heavy snow flakes

falling on the hills and fields.

삼월의 거리

봄비 개이며 산에서 들에서
진달래 개나리 피어나고
나뭇가지 사이로 나는 박새들
지저귀는 소리에도 윤기가 돈다
세상 떠난 어버이들 어느새
자식들 기억에서 사라지고
사람이나 짐승이나 모두들 새롭게
태어나기 바쁘다
보아라 팽팽한 청바지와
짧은 치마 비집고
물오른 몸매 터져나오는
삼월의 거리 곳곳이 눈부시지 않은가
가을 산골짜기에 단풍 불붙고
눈과 얼음 겨울밤에 빛나듯
여름날의 어둠 밝히려고 벌써부터
거리와 광장 가득 넘치며
환하게 솟아오르는 젊은이들
이들은 바로 사람의 봄 아닌가

March streets

When the spring rain stops, in hills and fields

azaleas and forsythia bloom

while the chirping of the tits flying

between the branches is full of renewed luster.

Parents who have departed this life

abruptly vanish from their children's memories,

people and animals are all busy

being reborn anew.

Just look—how dazzling the March streets are,

with everywhere people wedged into tight jeans

and tiny skirts,

increasing girth bursting the seams.

Just as maple leaves blaze in autumn up mountain valleys,

as snow and ice gleam bright in winter nights,

the streets and squares are already now full to overflowing

with young folk intent on brightening up the summer
darkness,

bursting out brightly—

surely they are our human springtime.

세검정 길

북악터널 확장 공사가 한창이다
푹파음 산을 울릴 때마다
세검정 가던 옛길
가슴속으로 뻗어나간다
자두꽃 앵두꽃 활짝 핀 날이면
닥종이 만드는 냄새 썩은 굴비 같던 길
시냇물 징검다리를 건너면
능금나무 과수원
걷다보면 갑자기 산이 막아서던
좁은 골짜기 아름다웠지
돌이켜볼 겨를도 없이
신호등이 바뀌고
기억의 검은 터널로부터
매연을 뿜으며 화물 트럭과
버스 승용차들 앞다투어 달려나온다
추억을 단속하듯 곳곳에서
범칙금 딱지를 떼는 교통 순경들

Road through the hills

They're in the middle of widening Bugak Tunnel.
Every time the sound of blasting echoes through the hills
the old road I used to take at Segeomjeong
stretches out inside my heart.
On days when plum trees and engdu were in full bloom
that road, like a smell of mulberry paper being made or of
rotten fish,
crossing the stepping stones over the stream
to apple orchards then, walking a little further,
suddenly a wall of mountains used to rise blocking the way
ahead
with that little valley, how lovely it was.
The lights change,
leaving no time to gaze around,
and out of memory's dark tunnel
lorries come racing, pumping out clouds of exhaust fumes,
while buses and cars compete.
Here and there, policemen are handing out tickets
as if they were enforcing a crackdown on memories.

北海에서

언젠가 꼭 한번 보고 싶었던
바다
북해에 왔다
브리들링턴 북쪽 해안
깎아지른 암벽 아래로
파도가 손 흔들며 몰려왔다
어디서 본 그림인가
벼랑 위 전망대에서
느닷없이 비바람에 휩쓸려
난간 밖으로 떨어지는 순간
저 아래 아득한 바위 끝에
꾸겨진 옷뭉치 하나
그것은 바닷물에 젖은
나의 주검이었다

The North Sea

At last I had come to the sea
I longed to view sometime—
the North Sea.
Beneath the towering cliffs along the coast
north of Bridlington
the surf came thundering, waving its hands.
There's a painting I seem to have seen somewhere—
falling from a lookout at the top of a cliff
suddenly swept away by a stormy wind
lying crumpled at the tip of the rocks far below
a bundle of clothes
soaked by the sea—
my corpse.

대성당

161m 종탑 끝까지
그 많은 벽돌을 한개 또 한개
500년 동안
수직으로 쌓아올렸다
그 많은 벽돌공의 손끝으로
완공된 대성당에서
100년이 지난 오늘도 성스러운
미사를 올리고 있다
입구에서는 건축 노동자들이 머리띠 두르고
연좌 데모를 하는 중이고

The cathedral

For five hundred years

they piled brick on brick, all those bricks,

to the top of the 161 meter-high tower.

Inside that cathedral, completed one hundred years ago

by the finger-tips of all those masons,

today too holy Mass is being celebrated.

At the entrance, construction workers with headbands

are staging a sit-down demonstration.

뒤로 걷는 사내

벽돌담을 넘어 한 뼘쯤
자기 집 뒤뜰로 뻗은 이웃집 목련
나뭇가지를 전정가위로 싹둑 잘라버리고
앞마당에서 쓰레기를 태우는 사내
담을 넘어 옆집으로
퍼져가는 고약한 연기는 아랑곳없이
뒤로 걷기 연습에 열중하고 있다
건강에 좋다는 것이다

Man walking backwards

The magnolia next door having crossed the brick wall
by a span or so and invaded his back garden,
after slicing off every branch with pruning shears
the man is burning garbage in his front yard
and now, unconcerned about the noxious smoke
spreading over the wall toward the house next door,
he is absorbed in practicing walking backwards.
People say it's good for one's health.

동해로 가는 길

동해로 가는 길 곳곳에
바다가 있지
설악산 넓고 깊은 골짜기
바위와 나무와 돌
제멋대로 널려진 채
시냇물 흐르다 잦아들다
그대로 있지
서른세 해 전에 올라갔던 울산바위
우람하게 버티어 선 기암괴석도
있는 그대로 보기 좋군
바람이 머물다 가는 소나무숲
끊임없이 몰려와 허옇게
소리치는 파도
모두들 있는 곳이 제자리
제자리에 편안히 있는데
산을 깎아내려 길을 넓히고
바다를 메꾸어 도시를 만들어도
달려와서 푸근히 쉴 자리
우리는 찾기 힘들군

The road to the east coast

Here and there along the road to the east coast,

we glimpse the sea.

In the broad, deep valleys of Mount Seorak

rocks and trees and stones

lie scattered at random.

Streams flow then dry up

just as they used to.

On Ulsan Rock, the rocky crag I climbed thirty-three years back,

curiously shaped rocks rise majestically

just as they used to — good to see them.

The pine groves where breezes pause on their way,

the waves that come surging in, roaring white —

all in their proper place as they are,

all peacefully in their places

yet though mountains are flattened, roads widened,

the sea filled in, towns built

after speeding all this way

we have a hard time finding

somewhere cozy to rest.

Note: Mount Seorak is a lofty massif rising close to the east coast not far from the DMZ. It and the coast with its groves of pine trees are extremely popular tourist destinations, with terrible traffic jams. Ulsan Rock is a picturesque outcrop close to the road which can easily be climbed in a couple of hours.

우부드를 지나서

우부드* 장터로 가는 길
아랫도리만 조금 가렸을 뿐
벌거벗은 몸에
수직으로 숨막히게 쏟아지는
적도의 햇빛 온몸으로 받으며
이글이글 끓어오르는
아스팔트 위를 맨발로 걸어가는
늙은이 앙상한 골격에
단단한 마당발로
이승이 끝날 때까지 천천히
걸어갈 것만 같아
잊을 수 없었지 그리고
자꾸만 바라보았지
느닷없이 쏟아지는 열대의 소나기
파파야 광주리를 들고
추녀 밑으로 들어선 할머니
깊숙이 주름살진 얼굴에
초점 없는 눈길
바싹 마른 가죽 같은 살갗에
움직이는 시체의 손
아무래도 이 장터를 벗어나
황톳길 검푸른 숲을 지나

Beyond Ubud

Along the road leading to Ubud market,

only her lower body lightly veiled

otherwise naked

her whole body exposed to

the equatorial sunlight

as it poured vertically downward oppressively

walking along barefoot

on the scorching burning asphalt

one elderly figure, a gaunt frame

on broad hardened feet,

apparently intending to keep walking on

slowly until the end of the world

I could not forget

kept looking.

A tropical shower suddenly poured down

the old woman took shelter under a projecting roof

carrying papayas in a round basket

unfocussed eyes in a deeply wrinkled face

skin like parched dry leather

where a corpse's hand moved.

It was somehow as if, passing beyond the market town

crossing the dark green forest along an earthen track

어딘가 높은 산 너머에

그녀가 살아갈

이승이 따로 있을 것만 같아

somewhere over a high mountain,

there might be another world

where she could go and live.

끝의 한 모습

천장과 두 벽이 만나는 곳
세 개의 평면이 직각으로 마주치는
방구석의 위쪽 모서리가
가슴을 답답하게 한다
빠져나갈 틈도 없이
한곳으로 모여
눈길을 막아버리는 뾰족한 공간이
낮이나 밤이나
나를 숨막히게 한다
빗소리와 새들의 노래 들려오는 창문
산수화 한 폭 걸려 있는 넓은 벽
현등이 매달린 천장
이들이 마침내 이렇게 만나야 하다니
못 한 개 박혀 있지 않고
거미줄도 없는 하얀 구석에서
앞으로 갈 수도 없고
뒤로 물러설 수도 없는
꼭지점에서 멈추어
이렇게 끝내야 하다니
결코 바라보고 싶지 않은
낮의 한구석
그대로 눈길을 돌릴 수 없는
밤의 안쪽 모서리

One image of the end

The place where ceiling and two walls meet,

the angle at the top of any room's corners

where three surfaces meet at right angles

fills my breast with feelings of anxiety.

That tapering space with no escape

all converging in a single point

blocking my line of sight

by day and by night

leaves me feeling breathless.

That window through which I hear rain falling, birds singing,

that spacious wall with a landscape painting hanging on it,

that ceiling with the light dangling from it—

the fact that these are forced to meet like that

in a corner where there's not one spiders' web,

not a single nail hammered in

with no way of advancing further

no way of retreating back

stopping at the point—

that they have to end like that

in a corner by day

that I have no wish to look at

an inward angle by night

that I cannot take my eyes off . . . .

다시 떠나는 그대

전화를 자동 응답으로 돌려놓고
거실에는 야간 점등 장치를 켜놓고
가스를 잠갔나 두 번 확인하고
보일러는 18℃ 이하로 맞춰놓고
거실에 FM 음악 방송을 틀어놓고
현관문을 이중으로 잠근 다음
다시 한번 뒤돌아보며 집을
떠난 그대여
한번 떠나서 돌아오지 않는 하루 이틀 나흘…
세금을 내고 비워놓은 이 집이
얼마나 오랫동안 견딜 수 있을지
신문과 광고물이 금방 문앞에 쌓이고
검침원이 초인종을 누르다가 되돌아가고
옆집 개가 빈집을 향하여 짖어대고
우편함에 꽂힌 공납금 고지서가 누렇게 빛 바래
이 집이 비어 있음을 누가 모르겠는가
그래도 그대는 떠난다 다시는 돌아올 수
없을 것처럼 집안 단속을 하고
문을 잠갔나 확인하고
손때 묻은 세간 가득 찬 정든
집을 등뒤로 남겨놓은 채
손가방만 하나 들고 결연히 떠나서

Leaving again

You left the house

with one final glance behind

after setting the phone to automatic messenger

turning on the evening lighting system in the living area

checking twice that the gas was turned off

setting the boiler to below 18 degrees

turning off the FM music program in the sitting room

and double locking the front door.

A day passed after you left and did not return, another, a third ···

How long will this house be able to take it, that you vacated

with all taxes paid?

Newspapers and publicity fliers accumulate before the door

the meter-readers ring the bell then turn away

the next-door dog barks at the empty house

requests for contributions stuffed into the mailbox turn

yellow:

could anybody fail to realize that this house is empty?

Still, before you left you tidied up

as if to say your were leaving and not coming back

you checked that the door was locked

turning you back on the beloved house

full of household goods soiled by use

새 집을 찾는다 언젠가
그 집을 가득 채우고 다시
비어놓은 채 뒤돌아보며 집을
떠날 그대여
몇 번이고 망설이며 떠났다가
소리없이 돌아와 혼자서
다시 떠나는 그대여

you quit the house resolutely, carrying only a small bag

in quest of a new house

then once that house is full, one day once again you

will quit it and leave, with just a glance behind you.

You will leave several times, hesitating

then come back, without a word, alone

then leave again.

가진 것 하나도 없지만

가진 것 하나도 없지만
무명 바지저고리
흰 적삼에 검은 치마
맨발에 고무신 신고
나란히 앉아 있는
머슴애와 계집아이
사랑스럽지 않은가
착한 마음과 젊은 몸뚱이밖에는
아무것도 가진 것 없지만
이들이 부지런히 일하는 곳마다
땅에는 온갖 꽃들 피어나고
지붕에는 박덩이 탐스럽게 열리고
시원한 바람이 땀을 식히고
해와 달과 별들이 하늘에 가득하네
팔을 꽉 끼고 함께 뭉치면
믿음직한 두 친구
뺨을 살며시 마주 대면
사이 좋은 지아비와 지어미
아득한 옛날로 거슬러 올라가면
너와 나의 어버이
가진 것 하나도 없이 태어났지만
슬기로운 머리와 억센 손으로

Nothing of their own, but still . . .

They have nothing of their own—
only a cotton jacket and pants
or a white blouse and black skirt.
Sitting side by side,
their bare feet shod in rubber slippers,
farm-boy and girl—
aren't they loveable?
They have nothing of their own
apart from their kind hearts and youthful bodies
but wherever they work diligently
all kinds of flowers spring from the ground.
On the roofs, pumpkin flowers blossom delightfully
cool breezes dry sweat,
the sky is full of sun, moon and stars.
When they link arms and work together as one—
those two trustworthy friends,
when cheek lightly touches cheek—
husband and wife in harmony,
when I look back on those long-ago times—
your parents and mine
were born with nothing of their own at all
but just think of all they achieved through hard work

힘들여 이룩한 것 많지 않은가
어느새 여기에 와 앉아 있네
우리의 귀여운 딸과 아들

with prudent heads and strong hands.
Suddenly here they are sitting with us—
our darling sons and daughters.

조심스럽게

조심스럽게 물어보아도 될까……
역사 앞에서 한 점 부끄러움도 없다고
주먹을 부르쥐고 외치는 사람이
누구 앞에서 눈물 한번 흘린 적 없이
씩씩하고 튼튼한 사람이 하필이면
왜 시를 쓰려고 하는지……
아무런 부끄러움도 마음속에 간직하지 못한 채
언제 어디서나 마냥 떳떳하기만 한 사람이
과연 시를 쓸 수 있을지……
물어보아도 괜찮을까……

Cautiously

Perhaps if I ask very cautiously⋯

Someone who clenches his fists and proclaims

he has not the least cause for shame before the face of

history,

someone tough and vigorous who never once

shed tears before anyone—

why on earth would someone like that want to write poetry ⋯?

someone incapable of storing shame inside his heart,

always everywhere totally clear and above board—

would someone like that be able to write poetry⋯?

Is it ok for me to ask, I wonder ⋯?

처음 만나던 때

조금만 가까워져도 우리는
서로 말을 놓자고 합니다
멈칫거릴 사이도 없이
— 너는 그 점이 틀렸단 말이야
— 야 돈 좀 꿔다우
— 개새끼 뒈지고 싶어
말이 거칠어질수록 우리는
친밀하게 느끼고 마침내
멱살을 잡고
싸우고
죽이기도 합니다
처음 만나 악수를 하고
경어로 인사를 나누던 때를
기억하십니까
앞으로만 달려가면서
뒤돌아볼 줄 모른다면
구태여 인간일 필요가 없습니다
먹이를 향하여 시속 110km로 내닫는
표범이 훨씬 더 빠릅니다
서먹서먹하게 다가가
경어로 말을 걸었던 때로
처음 만나던 때로 우리는

When first we met

If we start to grow close, we
urge each other to use familiar language.
Once there's no room to move even—
—I say you're wrong.
—Hey, bail me out.
—Bastard. I'll murder you.
The rougher the language, the
closer we feel until at last
we grab each other by the throat,
fight,
kill one another.
Do you remember when
we shook hands on first meeting,
greeted one another in formal terms?
If we can only go rushing ahead,
incapable of ever looking back,
then there's really no need to be human.
The cheetah racing after its prey at 110kph
is a lot quicker.
We need gradually to go back
to when we approached one another shyly,
exchanged words in formal style—

가끔씩 되돌아가야 합니다

to when first we met.

Note: The Korean language has grammatical forms which clearly mark levels of hierarchical relationship. One major distinction is that between formal and informal styles and the progress of a relationship is often marked by a change from one to the other.

누가 부르는지 자꾸만

누가 부르는지 자꾸만

그 넓은 안쪽을 들여다보고

안절부절 둘레를 빙빙 돌다가

다시 건너편을 바라보고

누구에게 대답하는지 자꾸만

그 움푹한 안쪽을 들여다보고

안타깝게 손짓하다가

갑자기 방책을 넘어

안으로 뛰어 들어갔다

누구를 껴안으려는지 한껏

두 팔 벌리고

구르듯 비탈을 달려 내려가

산굼부리 한가운데로

사라져버렸다

아물지 않은 상처를 뚫고

누가 끌어들이는지 홀연

옛 땅의 핏줄 속으로

빨려 들어갔다

쫓기다 쫓기다 마침내

Who's calling, I wonder

Who's calling all the time?
You peered into that gaping crater,
nervously made a complete turn of it,
looked across at the other side again
kept peering into the hollow interior
waving a hand regretfully
as if replying to someone
then suddenly jumping over the fence
you leaped in
arms open wide
as if about to embrace someone
you went racing down the slope
and vanished
in the very middle of Sangumburi crater
piercing a still unhealed wound
you plunged into an ancient underground vein
as if someone was pulling you
into the place
where those who died

굴속에서 죽은 이들이

수풀로 뒤엉켜

살아 있는 곳으로

in the caves there after endless pursuit

entagled in thickets

live on.

Note: Sangumburi is one of the many extinct volcanic craters in the island of Jeju-do, off the southern coast of Korea. The years following Korea's Liberation from Japanese rule were marked by strong, sometimes violent ideological divisions within Korean society. Beginning on April 3, 1948 and until the end of the Korean War, Jeju-do was the scene of terrible purges in which many hundreds died. Many who sought refuge in the vents and caves beneath the craters were never seen again. Until recently it was forbidden to mention these events, the memories of which still fester.

똑바로 걸어간 사람

— 金榮茂(1944-2001)를 생각하며

단풍잎과 은행나무잎이 가을바람에 흩날리는 어느 오래된 절에서 그를 본 사람이 있다.

일주문을 지나서 사천왕문에 다다를 때까지 그는 직선을 그어 놓고 그 위를 밟으며 가듯, 곧바로 걷고 있었다는 것이다. 다리를 쩍 벌리고 여덟팔자걸음을 걷는 관광객들 틈에서, 그는 준수한 사슴의 모습처럼 환하게 눈에 띄었을 것이다.

그가 결코 직선으로 걷는 연습을 한 것은 아니라고 믿는다. 그렇지 않아도 그는 평생을 똑바로 걸어온 사람이기 때문이다.

속임수도 에움길도 모르고 오로지 한 길을 뚜벅뚜벅 걸어온 그는 그렇게 우리 곁을 지나갔다. 조금도 서둘지 않고 똑바로 걸어서 우리를 앞서더니, 어느새 까마득히 멀어지다가, 갑자기 사라져버렸다. 우리는 말을 잃고, 홀린 듯이 그쪽을 바라보았다. 아무런 자취도 보이지 않았다.

안타깝게도 우리는 그가 떠난 것을 너무 늦게 알았던 것이다.

나중에 어느 천주교 성지에서 여전히 꼿꼿한 자세로 걸어가는 그의 모습을 보았다는 사람도 있다.

언젠가 갑자기 그와 마주치게 되지 않을지, 헛된 희망을 품고, 우리는 오늘도 그를 뒤따라가고 있다.

낙엽을 밟고 가는 그의 발소리나, 그의 카랑카랑한 목소리가

He walked straight ahead
—A tribute to Kim Young–Moo (1944~2001)

Someone caught sight of him at an ancient temple, where maple and gingko leaves were flying free in the autumn winds.

He said he seemed to have drawn a straight line from the first gateway to the porch sheltering the Four Heavenly Kings, and to be walking along it, straight ahead. Amidst all the other visitors walking splay-footed with legs wide apart, he must have struck the eye like some delicate deer.

I am convinced he was not just practicising walking in a straight line. For he was someone who spent his whole life walking straight ahead.

Ignoring deceit or roundabout ways, he strode past us along a single path. Never hurrying, always just walking straight ahead, he finally grew remote, far off, then suddenly disappeared. Left without words, struck dumb, we gazed after him. There was no trace left.

Alas, we learned too late of his departure.

Later someone said they'd caught sight of him at some Catholic shrine, walking bolt upright as before.

Today, vainly hoping that one day we may suddenly come

저 앞에서 들려오기를 기다리는 마음 간절하다.

어쩌면 그것은 우리의 뒤쪽에서 곧바로 눈길을 걸어오는 젊은
목소리로 들려올지도 모른다.

face to face with him, we continue to follow after him.

Our hearts yearn to hear the sound of his feet on the fallen leaves, the sound of his high, clear voice coming from ahead of us.

Or perhaps we shall hear that as a youthful voice coming from behind us, walking straight ahead along a snowy road.

Note: A number of gateways stand along the path leading to major temples. The first is usually called Ilju-mun, a gate supported on a single row of pillars. Nearer the temple comes a larger structure, a porch sheltering, on each side of the passage through it, statues of two of the Four Heavenly Kings, gigantic mythical figures shown triumphing over demons.

시인소개

김광규는 1941년 서울에서 태어나 서울대학교 독어독문학과를 졸업했다. 1960년 대학교 입학 초년생으로 김광규는 4.19혁명대열에 참가했다. 이후 그는 1972~4년간 독일 뮌헨에서 3년 동안 수학했다. 중·고등학교 시절부터 글쓰기에 재능을 보여 그의 작품이 학교 문예지에 실리고 전국규모의 학생문학 컨테스트에서 최우수상도 수상하였지만, 정작 글쓰기를 다시 시작한 것은 독일에서 귀국 후 30대 중반부터였다. 그 때의 시들은 1975년 계간 『문학과 지성』지에 실렸고, 같은 해에 그는 Heinrich Heine와 Günter Eich의 시를 번역 출판하였다. 1979년 그의 첫 시집 『우리를 적시는 마지막 꿈』이 출판되었지만, 그 해 10월 박정희 대통령 암살을 둘러싼 정치적 억압상황 때문에 그의 시집은 판매금지조치 당했다. 김광규는 계속해서 『아니다 그렇지 않다』(1983), 『크낙산의 마음』(1986), 『좀팽이처럼』(1988), 『아니리』(1991), 『물길』(1994), 『가진 것 하나도 없지만』(1998) 등의 시집을 내었다. 1996년 그는 다양한 문학 주제에 관한 산문집인 『육성과 가성』(1996)을 출판했다. 그의 최근 시집 『처음 만나던 때』(2003)는 제11회 대산문학상 시 부문 수장작으로 선정됐다.

1980년 이후, 그는 한양대학교 독문학 교수로 재직하면서 『19세기 독일시선』(1980), Bertolt Brecht시선집(1985), Günter Eich 방송극선집(1986), Günter Eich 시집(1987) 등의 독일 작품을 번역했다. 제1회 녹원문학상(1981), 제5회 오늘의 작가상(1981), 제4회 김수영 문학상(1984), 제4회 편운문학상(1994) 등 한국의 주요한 문학상을 수상했다. 최근에는 독일의 언어문학 예술원에서 수여하는 프리드리히-군돌프-문화상(2006년)을 받았다. 그는 독일과 한국의 문학교류에 적극적으로 참여해 왔으며 독일, 오스트리아, 스위스의 여러 도시에서 시낭송회를 개최 했다. 이 외에도 3천명의 청중 앞에서 낭독한 Medellin(Colombia)세계 시 축제를 비롯하여 미국, 일본 등 다른 여러 나라에서도 시낭송회를 연 바 있다. 그의 회갑을 기념하여, 2001년에 『김광규 깊이 읽기』라는 이름으로 그의 작품에 대한 비평과 증언과 대담을 묶은 단행본이 출판되었는데, 이 책은 그의 작품에 관한 심도 있는 연구의 길잡이로 적합하다. 그의 작품에 대한 한국과 독일에서의 광범위한 참고목록은 위의 책 315~9페이지에 실려 있다.

1988년에 김영무(서울대 영문과 교수)가 김광규의 초기 시집 3권의 주요 작품과 비평적 에세이를 모아 『희미한 옛 사랑의 그림자』라는 시선집을 출판했다. 이 책은 Brother Anthony가 『Faint Shadows of Love』(1991)라는 제목으로 번역하여 영국의 Forest Books(London)에서 출판했다. 이 책은 1991년 대한민국번역문학상을 수상했다(지금은 절판되었음). 이 책을 바탕으로 정혜영이 1999년에 독일어 번역시집을 출판하여 2001년 같은 상을 수상했다. 그의 작품은 최근에 스페인어와 일본어로 번역되었다. 2005년에 『김광규 시선집』(Brother Anthony 번역)이 『The Depths of a Clam』이라는 제목으로 미국의 White Pine Press (Buffalo)사에서 출판되었다. 여기 이 책에 역재한 시편들은 위의 시선집에 실리지 않은 작품들 가운데서 골라 엮었다.

The Poet

Kim Kwang-Kyu was born in Seoul in 1941 and studied
German language and literature at Seoul National University. In
1960, early in his university career, he participated in the
demonstrations of the April Revolution that were repressed by
a tragic massacre on April 19, which led to the fall of President
Syngman Rhee. He later studied for three years in Munich
1972–4. Although he had discovered a talent for writing during
his middle and high school days, when his work had been
published in school magazines and even won a national prize,
he did not begin to write poetry after that until he was in his
mid-thirties and had come back from Germany. His first
published poems appeared in the review *Munhak gwa jiseong*
in 1975, the same year in which he published Korean translations of poems by Heinrich Heine and Günter Eich. In 1979 his
first volume of poems *Urireul cheoksineun majimak kkum* 우리
를 적시는 마지막 꿈 (The last dream to affect us) was published
but then virtually suppressed in the political tensions surrounding
the assassination of President Park Chung-hee in October that
year; a second volume *Anida, geurochi anta* 아니다, 그렇지 않
다 (No, it's not so) followed in 1983, a third *K'ŭnaksan ui
maeum* 크낙산의 마음 (The heart of K'ŭnaksan) in 1986, a
fourth *Jompaengi cheoreom* 좀팽이처럼 (Like someone fussing

and fretting) in 1988. There followed 아니리 *Aniri* in 1991, *Mulgil* 물길 (Waterways) in 1994 and *Gajin geot hanado eopchiman* 가진 것 하나도 없지만 (Nothing of their own, but still…) in 1998. In 1996, he published *Yukseong gwa gaseong* 육성과 가성(Voices natural and disguised), a collection of his essays and articles on a variety of literary topics. His most recent collection of poems, *Cheoeum mannateon ttae* 처음 만나던 때 (When first we met), was published in 2003 and received that year's Daesan Literary Award for poetry.

Since 1980 he has been a professor in the German department of Hanyang University and he has published translations of 19th century German poems (1980), of poems by Bertolt Brecht (1985), of radio dramas by Günter Eich (1986), and of poems by Günter Eich (1987). He has received a number of major Korean literary prizes for his poetry: in 1981 the first Nokwon Literary Award and the fifth Today's Writer Award; in 1984 he received the fourth Kim Su-Yeong Award. In 1994 he was awarded the fourth Pyonun Literary Prize. In 2006, he was awarded the Friedrich-Gundolf-Prize by the German Academy for Language & Literature. In recent years, he has been actively engaged in promoting literary exchanges between Korea and Germany and has given readings of his poetry in numerous cities in Germany, Austria and Switzerland. He has equally given readings in Japan, in the United States, and in Medellin (Colombia) where he read to a crowd of three thousand. To celebrate Kim Kwang-Kyu's sixtieth birthday, a collection of articles on his work was published in 2001 with the title *Kim Kwang-Kyu gipi ilkki* 김광규 깊이 읽기 (Kim Kwang-Kyu: Reading deeply) which constitutes the most important source for critical comment on his achievement. A comprehensive bibliography of other studies of his work in Korean and German can be found on pages 315-9 of this volume.

In 1988 the late Kim Young-moo (Professor of English, Seoul National University) published *Huimihan yetsarang ui geurimja* 희미한 옛사랑의 그림자 (Faint shadows of old love), a selection from Kim Kwang-Kyu's first three volumes of poems, with a critical essay. These were translated by Brother Anthony and were published by Forest Books (London) in 1991 with the title *Faint Shadows of Love*. The volume received the Translation Prize in the Republic of Korea Literary Awards for 1991. It is no longer available. A volume of German translations by Chong Heyong was published in 1999 and won the same award in 2001. Translations of his work have also recently been made into Spanish and Japanese.

In 2005, a selection of Kim Kwang-Kyu's poems translated by Brother Anthony was published in the United States by White Pine Press with the title *The Depths of a Clam*. The poems in this present volume are those that were not included there.

역자 소개

프랑스 초교파 수도원 테제 공동체의 수사 브라더 안토니(한국
명 : 안선재)는 1942년 영국에서 태어나 1980년부터 한국에서 거
주하였다. 서강대학교 교수로 영문학을 가르치면서 김영무와 함
께 김광규 시선집 외에도 고은의 〈나의 파도 소리〉와 〈만인보〉,
천상병의 〈귀천〉, 신경림의 〈농무〉, 김수영, 신경림, 이시영 시선
집을 영어로 옮겼다.

The Translator

Brother Anthony is a member of the Community of Taizé
(France). Born in Britain in 1942, he has lived in Korea since
1980. He is a professor in the English department of Sogang
University, Seoul. In addition to Kim Kwang-Kyu's *Faint
Shadows of Love*, Kim Young-Moo and Brother Anthony
together translated *The Sound of my Waves, Beyond Self, Little
Pilgrim* and *Ten Thousand Lives* by Ko Un, *Back to Heaven* by
Cheon Sang-Byeong, *Variations* by Kim Su-Yeong, Shin Gyeong-
Nim, and Lee Si-Yeong. Brother Anthony has published some
twenty volumes of translations from Korean.

『한국문학 영역총서』를 펴내며

한국문학을 본격적으로 번역하여 해외에 소개하는 일이 필요함을 우리는 오래 전부터 절실히 느껴 왔다. 그러나 좋은 번역을 만나기는 좋은 창작품을 만나는 것 못지 않게 어렵다. 운이 좋아서 좋은 번역이 있을 경우에는 또한 출판의 기회를 얻기가 쉽지 않다. 서구의 유수한 출판사들은 시장성을 앞세워 지명도가 높지 않은 한국의 문학작품을 출판하기를 꺼린다. 한국문학의 지명도가 높아지려면 먼저 훌륭하게 번역된 작품들이 세계적인 명성이 있는 출판사에서 출판이 되어 널리 보급이 되어야 하는데, 설혹 훌륭한 번역이 있다 하더라도 이 작품들이 해외에서 출판될 기회가 극히 제한되어 있어서, 지명도를 높일 길이 막막해지는 악순환을 거듭하는 것이 현실이다. 이런 현실을 타개하는 길은 좋은 작품을 제대로 번역하여 우리 손으로 책답게 출판하여 세계의 독자들에게 내놓은 데서 찾을 수밖에 없다. 이런 일을 하기 위해 도서출판 답게에서 『한국문학영역총서』를 세상에 내놓는다.

'답게' 영역총서는 한영 대역판으로 출판되며, 이 총서는 광범위한 독자층을 위하여 만들어진 것이다. 무엇보다도 이 총서를 통해 해외의 많은 문학 독자들이 한국문학을 알게 되기를 희망한다. 이 총서는 또한 국내에서 한국학을 공부하거나 영어로 번역된 한국 작품을 필요로 하는 영어 사용권의 모든 사람들과 한국문학의 전문적인 번역자들을 위한 것이기도 하다. 전문 번역인들은 동료 번역자들의 작업을 자신들의 것과 비교함으로써 보다 나은 새로운 번역 방법을 모색할 수 있을 것이다. 고급 영어를 배우

기를 원하는 한국의 독자들도 대역판으로 출간되는 이 총서를 읽음으로써, 언어가 어떻게 문학적으로 신비롭게 또 절묘하게 쓰이는지를 깨닫는 등 많은 것을 얻을 수 있을 것이다.

　아무리 말쑥하게 잘 만들어진 책이라도 그 내용이 신통치 않으면 결코 책다운 책일 수 없다는 자명한 이유에서, '답게' 영역총서는 좋은 작품을 골라 최선의 질로 번역한 책만을 출판할 것이다. 또한 새로운 번역자의 발굴과 격려가 이 총서 발간의 목적 가운데 하나이다. '답게' 출판사가 발행하는 이 총서가 한국문학 번역의 중요성을 다시 한 번 일깨우고, 문학 작품의 번역이라는 불가능한 꿈을 가능하게 하려는 번역자들의 노력에 보탬이 되기를 바란다. 이런 시도가 여러 가지로 유용하고 또 도전적인 것이 될 때, 더 나아가서는 잘 번역된 한국 작품의 전세계적인 출판 작업이 이루어지는 단초를 마련할 수 있을 때, 이 선구적인 계획은 진정으로 성공적인 것이 될 것이다.

김영무(1944~2001)

Series Editor's Afterword

Extensive translation of Korean literature for foreign readers has for many years been felt to be a pressing need. But to fall upon a good translation is much harder than to discern a good original work. If we are fortunate enough to secure a good translation, it is often very difficult to get it published abroad.

The major publishers of the western world are not yet prepared to run the risk of publishing works of relatively unknown Korean literature. Yet if Korean literature is to achieve worldwide fame, it first of all needs to be well translated, and then put into circulation throughout the world by those very publishers which are so reluctant to publish even good translations of Korean literature. It is a vicious circle : no publication without fame but no fame without publication. To save the situation, we should perhaps try to make available to readers abroad choice translations we ourselves have published in editions of high quality. The DapGae English Translations of Korean Literature series has been launched with this aim.

Each volume of the DapGae series will be a bilingual edition. We expect a wide-ranging audience for the series. It is our primary hope that it will help introduce many foreign readers to the world of Korean literature. The series is especially intended to serve English-speaking students enrolled in Korean literature courses, as well as those who may wish to compare their own translations with the translations of fellow translators in order to find new and better ways of translating. Korean readers studying advanced English can also benefit from reading these bilingual editions : the experience may help them to recognize the mystery of true mastery of the literary use of language.

However well designed a book may be, it cannot properly serve its purpose if the contents are mediocre. For that reason the DapGae series will strive to introduce to the readers of the world the best translations of the finest works of Korean literature. One of the objectives of the series is to find and encourage new talents in English translation. We hope that the DapGae English Translations of Korean Literature series will serve in some small way to refocus attention upon the importance of translating Korean literature into good English and to make possible the impossible dream of literary translation. This pioneering project will be a true success not only if it proves useful and challenging but also if it paves the way for the publication of fine translations of Korean literature on a worldwide scale.

Young-Moo Kim(1944~2001)

저자와
협의하여
인지 생략

상 행

지은이 | 김광규
옮긴이 | 안선재(안토니 수사)
펴낸이 | 東原 張少任
펴낸곳 | 답게

초판 인쇄 | 2006년 12월 5일
초판 발행 | 2006년 12월 10일

주   소 | 137-834 서울시 서초구 방배4동 829-22호
원빌딩 201호
등   록 | 1990년 2월 28일, 제 21-140호
전   화 | 편집 02)591-8267 · 영업 02)537-0464, 02)596-0464
팩   스 | 02)594-0464

홈페이지 : www.dapgae.co.kr
e-mail : dapgae@chollian.net

ISBN 89-7574-206-7

나답게 · 우리답게 · 책답게